Exposure of Evil

EXPOSURE OF EVIL

Janie Bolitho

Constable · London

For Jim Parsons
my husband and friend

First published in Great Britain 1998
by Constable & Company Ltd
3 The Lanchesters, 162 Fulham Palace Road
London W6 9ER
Copyright © 1998 by Janie Bolitho
The right of Janie Bolitho to be
identified as the author this work
has been asserted by her in accordance
with the Copyright, Designs and Patents Act 1988
ISBN 0 09 478860 X
Set in Palatino 10 pt by
SetSystems Ltd, Saffron Walden, Essex
Printed and bound in Great Britain by
MPG Books Limited, Bodmin, Cornwall

A CIP catalogue record for this book
is available from the British Library

1

'The back door was open, you went in, and when you were disturbed, you shot her.' DCI Ian Roper eased himself into a more comfortable position. His back ached but he was probably not alone in this. Once more he hammered home the repeated questions, now phrased as statements. There was still no response from Petesy French.

Two patrol officers had brought him in on a drunk and disorderly. Later had come the charge of unlawful possession of a firearm. That was then. That was before they knew that Jasmine Grant was dead. Shot dead. The weapon in Petesy's hold-all, a Heckler & Koch 9 mm automatic hand-gun, had been fitted with a silencer and had recently been fired. After the second shot the mechanism had jammed. According to Ronald Titmuss, ballistics expert, this was par for the course with a silenced automatic. 'She was damn unlucky. If she hadn't been so close she might still be alive,' Titmuss had commented when he had been handed the gun. 'Unless you're used to the things they ain't easy to handle.'

But Jasmine Grant, known to everyone as Jassy, was dead. And what made it worse, although everyone admitted that it should not have done so, was that Jassy had been married to Joff Grant. Police Constable Joff Grant. Jassy and Joff. Everybody knew them, everybody liked them. Even their names had a certain ring.

Petesy French had not yet been charged with murder because it was not until two hours after he had been picked up that the body had been discovered and at the time he was still in the cells sleeping it off. It was hard to give credence to the assumption that French was a killer but it certainly looked that way.

'Where did you get the gun?'

5

'I don't know.'

DCI Ian Roper leaned forward a little to ease his back. These were the first words their suspect had spoken, apart from stating his name and address. 'But you admit to owning it.'

'You found it on me.'

We're on our way, Ian thought. Even though the answer was inconclusive it showed the man was ready to talk. The tape in the recording machine still turned slowly but so far all it had logged were the names and positions of those present and the questions he and Detective Sergeant Markham had been asking. If the air-conditioning had not been fully operational Ian thought he might have passed out.

Peter French, aged twenty-four, mixed in the wrong company. He liked being called Petesy and, although he was unaware that his so-called friends used the name derisively, he may have committed the crime for no other reason than to impress them.

'You entered the house with the intention of stealing but you were interrupted. When you saw Mrs Grant you shot her.'

'No.' There was a pause. 'I don't know. I was going to the launderette.'

One step nearer, Ian thought as he stared into Petesy's bloodshot eyes. The atmosphere in the room was tense and filled with the stench of the suspect. When he was brought in he had been unable to stand up; two patrolmen had half carried him to the cells. The custody officer had searched his bag, which had been taken from him along with his belt and his shoes. Petesy had thrown up over the bunk when he was shaken awake and told he was needed to answer some questions. Now, huddled in a blanket because his clothes had been taken away for analysis, he was sweating out the alcohol, and along with it came the unmistakable smell of fear. But no one wanted to leave the room. It was Joff Grant's wife who was dead.

DCI Roper, DS Markham and the PC standing behind

them were revolted by Petesy French. Given a chance Ian Roper would have left the sergeant alone with him. Markham's means of intimidation did not include physical violence, only a silence which was far more terrifying. Ian saw that it would be difficult to be dispassionate when it was the wife of one of their own who was dead. Outside the room in which they had been confined for so long there wasn't a person who couldn't wait to hear that they had a confession. There was none of the usual bustle and banter. Even the secretaries were speaking in whispers. And, of course, they were all waiting to hear who had drawn the short straw, whose job it would be to tell Joff. He was on his way back from a fishing trip in Scotland. Joff was ambitious and had recently put in for a course on special operations. He wanted to move on, to live up to the respect he had already earned. There wasn't an officer who knew him who did not believe him capable of achieving almost anything. And now his wife was dead and Joff would lose out doubly. No one would risk sending a man with a strong reason for vengeance into such a potentially sensitive field. Thankfully he had travelled by train so there would be someone at Ipswich station to meet him. Had he driven he would have arrived home to find police vehicles parked outside his house and neighbours standing in the street.

'It was your gun that killed her.' Another statement, one which might or might not be true. Ian waited but Petesy had retreated back into his own world. The gun had been fired but until the two rounds had been recovered, either during the post-mortem or via the scene-of-crime team when they had finished at the house, they did not know for certain that it had killed Jassy. However, it seemed improbable that there were two gunmen running around. The town had expanded, almost outgrown itself, but it wasn't Glasgow and it wasn't Manchester, it was Rickenham Green in Suffolk, and there had not been a shooting here for a long time.

They had their man; all they needed was a confession or adequate proof to put him away. The former was unlikely and the latter, Ian suspected, was not going to be easy to get. Yet it ought to be, their man was an incompetent. Ian's eyes were drawn to the clock on the wall. A few more minutes and Petesy would be entitled to another break. This time food would have to be provided. If it was fish and chips from the canteen the stench in the room would be unbearable.

There were no windows, only the blank walls. For the past week the temperature had been soaring, over eighty degrees in the shade and no sign of letting up. Gardens were parched, customers from pubs spilled out on to the pavements and over everything was a film of grit, but even the fetid summer streets would have been preferable to remaining in the same room as Peter French for longer than was necessary.

Petesy lit another cigarette and held it between his yellow-stained fingers. Ian smoked, between the times when he had given up, but he did not know how their suspect could get through so many when he must have been suffering from a tremendous hangover. The break would be welcome for all of them. If Petesy had gone on a bender *after* he did the deed, then his memory of prior events might improve. If he had committed the offence whilst drunk he might never remember at all. Ian stood. His shirt was damp and stuck to his back. He closed his eyes in disgust before quietly telling the PC near the door that he would have him relieved immediately.

Markham also rose, with a faint creak from his leather jacket, an item of clothing he was never without. He possessed a metabolism that was envied. Neither cold in winter nor hot in summer, his body seemed to be under the same tight control as his emotions – although the consensus of opinion was that he did not have any.

Despite the air-conditioning there was no respite from the warmth in the corridor although the air was fresher. A humid draught washed over them as a door was opened then closed. There were few sounds: the clack of word processor keys, a ringing telephone, but no buzz of conversation from the secretaries using them. Jassy Grant was dead.

8

'His train's due in any minute now.'

Ian nodded. 'Brenda will cope.' Someone senior should have gone but Ian had talked it over with Superintendent Thorne and the chief superintendent and they had agreed to his proposals. Brenda had been the first detective on the scene; she had witnessed the horror at first hand. She had stared down at what had once been the face of a young woman she had vaguely known, then distanced herself. Apart from a slight loss of colour Detective Constable Brenda Gibbons hadn't flinched. But they all guessed what had been going through her mind, the comparisons she must have made. She and the victim were both attractive and almost the same age but one was dead and the other was part of a team allocated to find her killer. If Brenda was sublimating her feelings it was better she faced Joff Grant because it would help put things into perspective. It was Joff's loss, not hers, and he would need someone to lean on.

'Yes, sir,' was all Brenda had said when she had been called into the super's office and asked if she was prepared to do it.

The detectives working in the general office raised their heads when Ian and Markham entered but it was clear from their faces that French had given them nothing. They went back to their various tasks without speaking. The room was dim and cooler than elsewhere in the station. Vertical slatted blinds were pulled across the windows which ran the length of one wall and shaded the occupants from the sweltering sun. Someone coughed and papers rustled, a telephone rang and was answered quietly. A colleague's wife was dead.

'I don't think he did it.' Markham leant against the edge of a desk, his hands in his jacket pockets, his blue eyes colder than ever.

Ian sighed and mopped his forehead with a tissue then threw it into the nearest waste bin. He could almost feel the bags beneath his eyes. It was seven fifteen on a hot evening in late August but he felt as though he had been up all night.

He hated the heat and he hated violent death but more than that he hated himself, or, rather, his lack of will-power. He was not in a fit state to be dealing with this case but he could not have anticipated events. The previous evening Moira had gone out with a friend and Ian had accepted Doc Harris's invitation to join him at the Elms Country Club where the Doc was a member. They served beer but it was not cask conditioned and Ian refused to drink it because it played havoc with his insides. Unlike the Doc he was not a whisky drinker but he had sunk too much gin and tonic. Now he was paying the price and could almost sympathise with Petesy French, who must have consumed at least five times the amount Ian had.

'Why not?' Markham rarely expressed an opinion. In fact, he was renowned for his lack of social skills, preferring to say nothing rather than make inconsequential conversation. Therefore Ian was more than prepared to listen. The comment had not been made without good reason and, he had to admit, the longer he spent in French's company, the more he was beginning to believe it himself. He hoped they were wrong, that their suspect was not displaying the body language of guilt simply because he had no recollection of what he had done. He desperately wanted to be wrong.

'Two reasons. It isn't his style and there's no motive.' Markham shifted his position slightly, allowing Ian a glimpse of his uncompromising profile. The features were well defined and regular yet he was not handsome. His fair hair was cropped short – not because of the heat, it was the way he always wore it.

Ian nodded. Petesy French had a history of minor offences, mostly shop-lifting and one charge of theft of a bicycle. If he had made a more successful career out of house burglary they did not know about it.

'As far as we know, nothing was taken.'

'He panicked.'

It was the way they worked. One of them would make a suggestion, the other would try to explain it away, only in

Ian's case it was usually Detective Sergeant Barry Swan with whom these interchanges took place. They had not seen much of each other recently. The previous October Barry had sat the first part of the Police Promotion Examination Board inspector's exams. To Ian's dismay he had passed it. Naturally he wanted Barry to do well but, conversely, he did not want to lose him. On average two-thirds of candidates failed the second part; Barry was not one of them. And Barry Swan, whose son had been born three days ago, and whose promotion Ian had recommended, would now be leaving.

'There's nothing to place him in the house.'

'There's the weapon. It'll be the same gun.' Neither of them really doubted that.

'But did he fire it?'

'His prints are all over it. He was picked up not far from the house.' DCI Roper did not want to listen.

'Then scene-of-crime will find them there too.'

The room was quieter still as the other detectives stopped whatever they were doing to listen. French's prints were on the gun but not, as Ian had said, all over it. There were smudges where it might have been handled by someone else. Where the gun came from was a question which could wait. It was all too easy to purchase a firearm if you knew the right people. 'Come on, let's get some coffee.'

Together they went down to the basement cafeteria. Hot food was on display beneath copper-coloured lamps. Since the heatwave had begun little of it was sold. They ordered coffee and sat at one of the formica-topped tables with its brightly coloured plastic chairs. The place reminded Ian of his school gym – it had doubled as a dining-room, which, he thought, wouldn't be allowed now. He felt the questioning glances of the few other people present and ignored them.

'Once more then we'll leave him to stew.'

Markham nodded and poured sugar from the dispenser into his coffee. They would be able to hold him without charging him. Under the circumstances an extension would almost certainly be granted.

11

Allowing French enough time to eat whatever had been sent up from the canteen, they returned.

The tray was still on the table. Ian indicated for it to be removed. The PC now guarding their suspect picked it up and placed it on the floor outside the door then returned to his seat where French could see him but Ian and Markham could not.

Petesy French belched quietly into the back of his hand. Ian thought it a rather refined gesture for such a man. The tray had contained a cup and saucer and a plate on which rested an empty plastic sandwich container. French, too, was feeling the heat but he looked marginally better now that he had eaten.

Ian reset the tape and they began again. 'Tell us about your day.'

'What?' Petesy's head jerked up just as he was about to light a cigarette. The match burned half-way down. He was taken aback at the DCI's bland expression and this new conversational tone of voice. 'I don't understand what you mean.'

'Assuming you went to bed last night, you got up this morning, then what did you do?'

Petesey's eyes narrowed in concentration. 'I had a wash, put the kettle on then went down the paper shop.'

'In Deben Road?'

'Yeah. That's where I live, isn't it?'

They knew that, of course. Deben Road was on the large council estate which sloped gently up one of the few hills in the area. When that estate and other, private estates had been built the councillors in office at the time had decided to name the new streets after Suffolk rivers. Deben Road had been sold off under the Right to Buy scheme. 'What did you buy?'

'The *Sun*, and half an ounce of tobacco. You can ask Jack's missus, she always serves me.'

'Did you have the gun with you then?'

'Of course not.'

'What next?'

'I went home and made a pot of tea and read the paper. Then I picked out my horses. If there's racing I do an accumulator. You never know, do you?'

Markham glanced at Ian, who knew what he was thinking. French was suddenly willing to talk and, more importantly, his memory seemed unimpaired. They would check his every movement, though, because if this was his usual routine he might be confabulating.

Petesy French squinted through the smoke and removed a strand of tobacco from his lower lip. 'As soon as the betting shop opened I went in.' He grinned and reached beneath the blanket before remembering he wasn't wearing his jeans. 'In my jeans,' he said, 'You'll find the ticket there.'

Markham left the room to check. Amongst French's possessions was a betting slip, timed and dated by computer. The bet had been placed at ten twenty-five that morning. Markham and Ian both knew that French was not clever enough to have found it and kept it to use as an alibi later.

'I wonder if any of them've come in,' said French with a wan smile.

'After you placed your bet at ten twenty-five, where did you go?'

'Stayed in the bookie's for a bit chatting to a bloke who's often there when I am. Can't tell you his name, but the lad behind the counter'll bear me out. At opening time I went down the Black Horse.'

That hell-hole in Saxborough Road, Ian thought, as he pictured the fruit machines and video games with their flashing lights and bursts of theme tunes. Since the Prince William had changed hands and its name and become respectable, the small-time villains, fences and informants had relocated to the Black Horse. Obligingly the landlord had equipped it in what he believed to be their taste, including banks of screens over the bar where videos of pop singers could be seen as the music played on the juke-box. In Ian's opinion he had wasted his, or the brewery's, money because his new clientele had been quite happy in the squalor of

13

the Prince William where there had been no technological entertainment apart from an ancient fruit machine in the passage which had led to the Gents. Without any need for words Ian knew that Markham had clocked that last statement. DS Markham was at his best when out on the streets where he was often mistaken for a villain himself. He understood their mentality and he had more informants than anyone else. If there was anything to be gleaned from that insalubrious pub, Markham would find it. There was also the possibility that it might have been before eleven when French entered those hallowed portals: the landlord had a short memory when it came to the licensing laws.

'You stayed there until when?' What was puzzling was how he could have got so drunk so quickly. It was a few minutes after 1 p.m. when he was picked up. Two hours, give or take, for someone of French's capacity for drink did not seem long enough, but he might have been topping up from the night before. The idea made Ian feel nauseous.

'Ah, well, you see, I can't help you there. You'd have to ask someone who saw me leave. Last thing I remember is falling over in the Gents, next thing is I'm here enjoying the hospitality of one of your cells.' He ground the thin, soggy cigarette end into the ashtray.

He had been brought in and left to sleep it off. At ten past three, when the discovery of Jassy Grant's body had been reported, he had been rudely awakened, stripped and brought to the interview room. Naturally he was a suspect: there was the gun and the fact that he had been found, crashed out in some long grass, not far from Jassy and Joff's house.

Ian nodded at Markham, indicating that he was to take the lead, but a fresh approach produced nothing. French was taken back to the cells where, it appeared, all he wanted was twelve hours' uninterrupted sleep. He refused the offer of a solicitor and seemed indifferent to the fact that he was being held overnight. Maybe he was relieved that the temptations of the Black Horse would be out of his reach for once.

Markham left the building. He would call in at that same establishment on his way home. Ian remained at the table, his head aching, his thoughts unclear, but after ten minutes he, too, left.

Moira Roper was sitting at the kitchen table surrounded by books and papers. The back door was wide open and through it a huge orange sun could be seen sinking behind the copper beech at the bottom of the garden, turning its leaves to fire. The garden was fresh as she had carefully watered the flowers with a can, mindful of yet another hosepipe ban. The rich perfume of the nicotiana beneath the window filled the room.

She was wearing pale blue jeans and a short-sleeved white shirt. Her feet were bare and her shoulder-length blonde hair was held back in a pony-tail.

Ian left his car in the road and came around the side of the house, smiling when he saw her engrossed in her books. She looked so very young. Compared with himself, she was; fifteen years younger, in fact, but most people would have underestimated her age by ten years. She looked cool and clean and lovely, the perfect antidote to the dirt of the day. 'How's it going?'

Moira started. 'Ian! I didn't hear you.'

'I wish you wouldn't leave the door open when I'm not here,' he said irritably, stooping beneath its lintel.

'Oh, don't be silly. Half the time I'm out in the garden anyway. What's the difference?'

Good question, he thought. But somehow being inside with a door open seemed to place a person in a more vulnerable position than if they were outside.

'Anyway, this isn't going so well at the moment.' She indicated the paperwork. 'I just can't get my head around tort.'

Ian was not overjoyed that his wife was taking a law course but he did not let her know it. It was fear, on his part, because over the last five or six years and, more recently, since their son Mark had left home, she had shown less and less interest in the domestic things she used to enjoy, or he had believed she had enjoyed, and was becoming more independent both financially and intellectually. He was beginning to feel that she had overtaken him and that all he had left was the years until his retirement. His fear was that then he would no longer have anything to offer her.

There were no classes at the moment but Moira spent an hour or so most days studying, sometimes at the garage where she worked if they were quiet. He made no comment but pulled open the fridge and enjoyed a second or two of pleasure as the cold air briefly enveloped his legs. Reaching for the two-litre plastic bottle of Adnams he instantly recalled the excesses of the previous night and chose milk instead. He drank straight from the carton and felt the cold liquid trickle down his throat as Moira cleared away her papers.

Two plates of fresh salmon salad sat in the fridge. Moira got them out and removed the film covering them. As she laid the table she said, 'I'm going over to see Lucy tomorrow. Do you want to come?' Smiling, she shook a bottle of low-fat salad cream then placed it next to the salt and pepper. She had known Barry Swan for a long time, since his womanising days, and she had been as surprised as everyone else when he had married the dark-haired, intelligent, assertive Lucy who was a far cry from the clinging leggy blondes to whom he had always been attracted. And now, after a miscarriage, they finally had a three-day-old, eight-pound son, as yet unnamed. It was hard to reconcile Barry with parenthood.

'No. I don't think I can.'

'Ian?' Moira stood behind her chair, her hands resting on the back of it.

'Jassy Grant's been shot. She's dead.'

'Oh, no! Oh, poor Joff.' But beneath the horror she also understood what Ian was saying, that there was no telling when he would be free for social visits.

They ate in subdued silence. Moira knew that at some

16

point he would want to talk; when he was lacking in progress, when he needed a sounding-board or when he was genuinely interested in her opinion. That time was still some way off. For now, along with his food, he had to digest the fact that someone he had known had been murdered.

Moira, too, had known Jassy but only as an acquaintance. They had not been to the wedding, which had taken place four years ago, but they had received an invitation to the party in the evening which had followed the reception and they had met since at various police functions. For a young PC and his wife the wedding had been quite an affair but Jassy's parents had funded the whole day and, if what rumour decreed was true, then the expenditure would have meant little to them. What saddened Moira was that Joff and Jassy had not had a chance as a couple, their adult lives had barely begun. She had a good marriage and a son of whom she was proud: Mark, twenty-two years old and living in Italy whilst he painted and decided what he finally intended doing with his life now that he had completed art college. She never mentioned to Ian that she found it incredible that their son was now grown up and capable of looking after himself in a foreign country. She had relinquished mother-hood gradually since Mark had left school, but always with reluctance. Jassy would not have the opportunity to discover the ups and down of it.

The lack of conversation made Moira uneasy but experi-ence had taught her that the most expedient way of getting Ian to talk was to remain silent herself.

DC Brenda Gibbons felt the heat as much as everyone else but managed not to show it. She was dressed in a straight skirt of apple green, a white cotton blouse and low-heeled sandals. Her long hair, a shade somewhere between brown and chestnut, was tied loosely back in a scarf. A few stray wisps framed her face. She might have just stepped from the shower. But Brenda Gibbons had had a long day and it was not yet over and she felt unclean, inside and out. Her tanned legs were bare but she could hardly wait to step out of the rest of her clothes and into a tepid bath. The elastic at the edges of her bikini briefs chafed where sweat had dried, sweat not totally due to the high temperatures.

The sight of Jassy's body had been one thing, having to tell Joff would be another matter. Violent death and blood did not affect her the way they did some of her colleagues. Her own disastrous childhood, compounded by a violent marriage, had inured her to most things. But she had spotted the pattern of her life and changed it. Having left one destructive home for another, she had to break free of the cycle. Just when Harry thought he had crushed her, when he had slapped her once too often and been caught out in another affair, Brenda had packed his bags and sent them to his brother's house. A taxi had come to collect them almost at the same time as a locksmith handed her a new set of keys to the house. She saw a solicitor that same afternoon. She had expected some form of revenge but it had not come. Harry, it seemed, was a true bully, lost when power was taken away from him.

Now she was used to living alone and was beginning to enjoy making the decisions which had previously been denied to her. One day she saw quite clearly what it was about her that made certain people react as they did. She frightened them. She was a paradox. Despite her subordination in her home life she had systematically overcome all obstacles which related to school and career. Harry was not a man to allow any woman to outdo him but he had finally misjudged her.

All this passed through her mind as she headed towards Ipswich and Joff Grant's train. Anything rather than think about the news she was about to deliver. The journey was awful; the car was sticky, the radio crackled and she had managed to coincide with the rush-hour traffic which was filling the air with noxious fumes.

Andrew Osborne was nothing like Harry. She had met him

18

several months ago. A solicitor. The opposition. Except that he specialised in personal injury claims and therefore they were unlikely to come face to face in a courtroom. Because of what lay ahead of her Brenda had had to cancel a date with him that evening. He had said he understood. She hoped he meant it because that was the way things were with her job.

Braking suddenly, she waited for a car to vacate a parking space ahead of her. Ipswich had almost finished disgorging its commuters but heat and fumes still hung heavily in the air. Even the pigeons were lethargic as they strutted around seeking crumbs.

There were fifteen minutes before Joff's train was due. Brenda prayed it was on time because the waiting was unbearable. A note pinned to the cork board in Jassy's kitchen indicated that she had intended meeting him herself.

Brenda stood where she could watch the passengers alight. Nervously she chewed her thumbnail as the train's headlights came into view. Everything seemed to happen in slow motion. It approached sedately and ground to a halt with a hiss of brakes. There was a pause before the door catches were released. Finally the passengers began to step on to the platform. Brenda was holding her breath, waiting for the familiar figure to appear. She was oblivious to the bustle and noises all around her: the pushing people, the slamming of train doors and the announcements concerning arrivals and departures. Travellers surged towards her, singly or in pairs. Most carried briefcases, some had luggage. For one hopeful moment she thought Joff had taken another train and she would not have to be the one to break the news. Then she saw his dark head and the tips of the canvas-covered fishing-rods which he carried against his shoulder like a soldier carries a gun on parade. Joff was walking briskly towards her, scanning the crowd.

'Brenda?' He would have walked right past her had she not touched his arm. He was expecting Jassy to have been there. 'What is it? Has something happened?'

Brenda inhaled deeply. It was unreal. Nothing this awful could be happening on the concourse of a station at the tail end of the rush hour. 'It's bad news, Joff.'

He dropped his hold-all to the ground and she saw that it was pointless suggesting they went somewhere quieter. Joff wanted to know why she was there in place of his wife. 'It's Jassy, isn't it? She's had an accident.' A deep frown creased his sunburned brow but there was pain and pleading in his sea green eyes. He grabbed his bag and began to move towards the exit. 'Where is she? Rickenham General?' he called over his shoulder.

'Wait! Please!' Brenda hurried after him. 'Please, wait a minute.' Allowing the last few straggling passengers to pass she said, 'Jassy's been shot. She's dead, Joff.' For a couple of beats Brenda felt nothing. The enormity of what she had said hit her at the same time as Joff's brain registered the words. As if a minor earth tremor had passed beneath where they stood, her knees buckled momentarily and Joff swayed a little. You're on duty, Brenda reminded herself. This is all part of the job. But she still felt sick. How much worse must her colleague be feeling? For both their sakes she needed to act as if the whole scenario was unconnected with anyone she knew. Bending over, she picked up the hold-all. It was not heavy. With one hand beneath Joff's elbow she guided him out of the station and to where she had parked the car. Unlocking it she nudged him into the front passenger seat then she put his belongings into the back, almost having to tug his rods from his hand. Then she got in the car herself. Joff had not said a word since he had heard the news.

'Joff?'

Brenda reached across and touched his arm but he flinched so violently that she pulled her hand back. He was shaking his head.

'No. Not Jassy. Not my lovely Jassy.' He turned to face Brenda, who had to swallow back her own tears when she saw his running down his face.

'It's true. I'm so sorry.' She wanted to start the car and drive him back to Rickenham Green where there would be other people to take some of the burden from her but she was ashamed of the thought. It was selfish. Besides, she was not yet certain of his state of mind. She dared not risk him doing something crazy like throwing himself from the car whilst they were moving.

'Who did it? I'll kill the bastard. So help me God, I'll kill him.' The tears started in earnest. Joff leant against the padded dashboard, his head in his arms, and wept.

Thank you. Thank you. Brenda offered a silent prayer to whoever might be listening. Real grief at last, and anger. That was a healthy sign.

'Sorry.' Joff raised each arm in turn and wiped his eyes in the shoulders of his short-sleeved shirt. 'I want to see her. Let's go.'

'OK.' Brenda indicated and pulled out into the traffic. A car stopped and flashed its lights to enable her to do so. Joff would be asked to make a formal identification although there was no doubt that the victim was his wife. Jassy's abundant hair, the colour and texture of wheat, had been spread out on the floor, streaked with blood, and worse. Her perfect shape and distinctive clothes were another marker, but bodies had been switched before and in this case the face was unrecognizable. Brenda could not tell him that. She drove slowly to allow her own emotions a chance to settle down. As they neared Rickenham Green Joff asked abruptly, 'Have you got a suspect?'

'Petesy French.'

She risked a sideways glance. Joff merely nodded, his face grim. 'Who found her?'

'A friend. Sally Foster?'

Joff nodded again. 'I want to go straight to the station,' he said a few minutes later as they came up to the roundabout at the end of the dual carriageway.

'Sure?'

'Positive.'

Brenda turned left. He would not be allowed anywhere near French, nor would he be involved in the case. Superintendent Thorne would see to it that Joff was on immediate compassionate leave, for all their sakes, as well as his own. If personal considerations were at stake, especially ones as great as these, an officer could be a danger to everyone or, at the very least, a hindrance.

They pulled into the newly resurfaced car-park. There were indented tyre marks where the tar had melted in the heat and it was sticky beneath their feet. They walked towards the building with the pungent smell of warm bitumen in their nostrils.

Now that the shops across the road had closed and the traffic was light the calmness of a summer's evening descended upon them. But it offered no peace. A bird began to sing, high up in one of the leafy trees which helped to disguise the modernity of the police station: four melancholy repetitive notes.

Brenda escorted Joff up to the superintendent's office. Mike Thorne, as supportive as always, had promised to wait until they returned, no matter how late it was. He stood when he heard the knock and told them to come in. 'I'm sorry, Joff. I don't know what else I can say.' He extended his hand. It was a second or two before Joff took it. Over his shoulder Mike Thorne raised his eyebrows in a question. Brenda nodded. Yes, Joff knew his wife had been shot. 'Thank you, DC Gibbons. You can go home now.' By giving her her rank he was reinforcing what she had told herself earlier. It was all part of the job.

'Yes, sir.' She walked quickly away, sensing many eyes on her as she headed straight for the exit. But no one spoke to her, just as no one had spoken when she and Joff had walked in, heading in the opposite direction. Condolences would come later, when Joff Grant had had time to get used to the idea. Thorne was probably aware that her spell of duty was not quite complete but he had kindly spared her the questions

22

she was bound to be subjected to if she hung around. One day she would thank him.

At home, in the modern terraced house she had shared with Harry, she poured a Campari and soda, one of the few alcoholic drinks she enjoyed. She opened all the windows and sank into a chair. There was no breeze; the curtains hung limply from their rail. Unconsciously she allowed her thoughts to travel where they would.

The house had not been her choice – she would have preferred something with more character – but it had been all they could afford and it had the advantage of being easy to keep clean. Not long ago she had bought Harry out. It had taken every penny she could lay her hands on but it had been worth it, and now she was making her own mark, painting the walls and moving furniture around. The contrast with the Grants' house was enormous. They lived in a road leading off Maple Drive. The area consisted of detached and large semi-detached properties, and any of the roads bisecting Maple Drive or Maple Grove was an enviable place to live and a most desirable address.

Trees and rivers, Brenda thought inconsequentially, although it was in the poorer areas that the streets had taken their names from the rivers. Aspen Close: the Grants' address. There were still a few of those trees surviving. There had been catkins in the spring. How would it feel to live in a house with four bedrooms, two reception rooms and a kitchen and bathroom to die for? She bit her lip. It was not a good choice of phrase. She had, of course, seen the whole of the place once the relevant teams had arrived at the scene and begun their painstaking work. They had found nothing unusual, no forced entry, no overturned furniture or the contents of drawers flung about. The house was a mock Tudor affair, although more tastefully done than some she had seen. There were leaded windows and beams but the decor was light and airy. Of course, everyone knew that Jassy had money behind her.

The kitchen was the only room not decorated in pastels. The units were of a dark wood and the gleaming door of the cooker which was set into the wall was a deep red which matched the cushion flooring. And Jassy's blood which had spread across it.

It was there that her body had been discovered by a friend. As soon as Mrs Sally Foster had been calmed sufficiently to speak coherently she had been questioned. She would be questioned again tomorrow. As confirmed by Jassy's diary, her visit had been pre-arranged. She had ... 'No more,' Brenda said aloud, standing up to refill her glass. Allowing her thoughts to wander only took them back to the one subject she was trying to avoid.

She slipped a classical CD into the player, Dvorak, and turned the sound up high, but not too high to bother the neighbours.

In her own small kitchen, where she could touch every surface and cupboard if she stood in the middle, she made a cheese and Marmite sandwich, adding lettuce and tomato at the last minute because it was time she consumed a few vitamins. It was also time she ate a proper meal. But not tonight.

2

Detective Sergeant Barry Swan had watched the birth of his son despite his intentions to the contrary and the fact that Lucy had stated she would rather he wasn't there. He had planned to stay with her until the last minute, offering support or holding her hand or whatever other useless things fathers were supposed to do. However, events had overtaken them. The baby had been in a hurry and when Lucy, through gritted teeth and between pants, had said, 'Will you please sod off,' it had been too late. He had stood at the head of the delivery couch, mesmerised.

'Phew. Thank Christ that's over,' were Lucy's first words of motherhood whilst Barry had sunk into his chair, stunned beyond belief at what he had witnessed and more emotional than he had thought possible.

Lucy had been handed the child. She studied him for a moment or two then turned to Barry, smiling when she saw tears glistening in his eyes. She patted his hand. 'There, there, it's all over now.'

But Barry was still unable to get over it. Lucy had been in hospital for three days. After the miscarriage last year the medics were taking no chances. If tomorrow's tests on mother and baby were satisfactory he was going to collect her in the afternoon. To everyone's amazement Barry had applied for paternity leave. He was a little amazed himself.

He had put in half a shift that day so was aware of Jassy Grant's death. Knowing what it was likely to do to Joff he felt bad, but nothing could quell his own joy. Other events taking place in the world seemed of little importance.

Because there would be fewer opportunities for a night out after tomorrow, Barry had left the maternity unit as soon as his son was asleep and his wife's eyelids were beginning to droop. He went to the Crown but there was no sign of Ian. After one drink he cut down the alley leading to the High Street and walked to the top of it. Opposite was St Luke's church, once the focal point but now dwarfed by Fine Fare. On his right was the Feathers where many of his colleagues chose to drink. There were a couple of faces he recognised but none of the usual crowd. Andrew Osborne, the solicitor, was sitting glumly in the corner nursing a pint. Barry grinned. Brenda must have stood him up. It was one of life's ironies that, when he had something to celebrate and was prepared to pay for the drinks, there was no one around to appreciate it. He decided to take himself to the Taj Mahal. After all, he had his promotion to celebrate too.

This meant walking back down the High Street. A small crowd was coming out of the cinema after the early evening performance of one of the three films showing. The matinée had been a Walt Disney, in deference to the school holidays. It would not be long before they were taking their son to such films. Three adolescents, all male, hung around outside the kebab place debating whether or not they had enough to get something to eat. His son would never be in that position. How different the world looked from the standpoint of fatherhood. There were so many dangers to be overcome he wondered how they would cope.

The door of the Taj Mahal was jammed open with a wedge of wood but it was still warm inside. Barry was welcomed with the cordiality due to a regular customer. Only a couple of tables were occupied but it was not surprising. At the weekends, and around pub closing time, was when it got busy. Nine thirty was early for him to be ordering a curry. Without needing to, he surveyed the menu. Whilst he did so a pint of lager appeared without him having to ask for it. He hung his lightweight jacket over the back of the chair and pulled at the knees of his loosely cut trousers so as not to spoil the creases. Then he rolled up his sleeves.

The work he had attended to over the last few days mostly consisted of preparing files for the DPP. Everyone was aware of his impending paternity leave and knew of his application for a transfer so did not consider it worthwhile for him to become involved in anything new. Having decided what he wanted to eat he ran a hand through his pale, thinning hair, which he wore swept back from his forehead, and looked for a waiter. As he did so the light from the candle in its brass and red glass holder caught the gleam of the fair hair on his forearms.

'I'm ready,' Barry said as one approached; his stomach was responding to the aromas wafting out from the noisy kitchen. The waiter smiled, his pen poised over a pad. 'One plain rice, one prawn dansak, one onion bhaji, one dhal and a nan, please.'

26

The waiter nodded and wrote it down, repeating it back as he did so. The detective had over-ordered as most customers did, but as long as they paid, it didn't matter. Of course, he was often accompanied by the chief inspector who had never been known to leave anything.

Barry sipped the lager, his hunger growing every minute. At last the hot plates arrived, then the food itself. He heaped most of it on to his plate and ate quickly. As always, he began to feel full too soon and had to slow down, signalling to the waiter to bring him another lager.

'Everything all right, sir?'

'Fine, thank you. Excellent as always.' He struggled with the meal for a bit longer before he realised he was not going to be able to get through it. Pushing his plate away he stretched then lit a cigarette. Unlike Ian he had no intention of giving up but he could, he had discovered since visiting Lucy at the hospital, go for long stretches without one. He intended not smoking in the presence of . . . James? Matthew? Mark? No, Ian's son was called Mark. Everything he thought of was either too ordinary or too biblical, although most names would go with Swan. Something fashionable or made up, as some names seemed to be now, might become out-dated or liable to ridicule when the child got older.

With nothing but thoughts of his son on his mind Barry picked up his jacket and left the restaurant, pleased that he had to walk home because his stomach was full.

The air was still humid but after the restaurant it felt cool. He had strolled to the corner, his hands in his pockets, when a jolt of memory sent the blood rushing into his face. He had walked out of the Taj Mahal without paying.

Retracing his steps he hurried back. The waiter who had served him gave him a funny look, as did Mr Ali, the owner, who was standing behind the counter where the takeaways were served.

'Look, I'm really sorry. I just wasn't thinking. You see, we've just had a baby.' Feeling even more foolish because he was about to do something he disliked in others, he produced several Polaroid shots of the child taken just after his birth. 'My son.'

'Ah, Mr Swan. Congratulations. Very well done, sir.'

'We haven't decided on a name yet.'

Mr Ali nodded, then hesitated for a second before saying, 'You have the meal with us.'

'No. It's kind of you, but here.' He slid a credit card out of his wallet.

'No. No. for the baby.' Mr Ali waved both hands as if he was shooing away an unwelcome dog.

'I insist.' Barry looked up but could not decipher the expression on the owner's face. Mr Ali shrugged, picked up the card and turned his back to run it through the machine.

Anyone else could have accepted the offer, especially on the strength of the amount of money Barry had put into the till, but he could not risk Mr Ali telling people of his generosity; Barry was a member of the CID and such a gesture might be misunderstood.

Making his way home for the second time he felt more relaxed than he had done for a long while. The miscarriage, Lucy's depression, worries at work, it was all in the past. His only thought now was of having Lucy and his son home. Alex? Andrew? Angus? Too pleasantly tired to think, he decided to let Lucy choose. By the time he let himself into their flat he had forgotten all about the embarrassing incident at the Indian restaurant.

Joff Grant could not have gone home had he wished to. The forensic team had not finished and were likely to be there until quite late, according to John Cotton who was head of scene-of-crime. Fingerprint dust was everywhere but PC Grant would be spared that ordeal. His prints were already recorded.

Superintendent Thorne made several suggestions as to where he might spend the night, including the police flats at the back of the station, but they were all rejected.

'Would you like someone else to inform your parents? And your wife's family?' Thorne had conscientiously consulted the personnel file because he did not want to put his foot in it if one or other of Joff's parents were no longer around. 'Would you rather do it yourself?' he persisted in his Birmingham accent which time had not diluted.

'I'll let my parents know. But Jassy's . . . no, I can't do that. There's her sister, too.'

'It's all right. We'll take care of it.' Thorne's face was pale despite the long hot summer, and the top of his head, now completely bald, shone under the light bulb. It was not yet dark although dusk was gathering and a few small clouds which had drifted out of nowhere were turning pink at the edges. Thorne had switched on the lights, wanting to dispel the gloom in advance. He was a tallish man – although still several inches shorter than DCI Roper who towered over everyone – and inclined towards pudginess, a fact he managed to conceal beneath suits which were just a little too big for him. He disliked the heat because it made his skin red and his head peel unless he wore a hat.

The offer to contact Jassy Grant's parents was not as altruistic as it may have seemed. If Petesy French was innocent everyone who had formed part of the circle of Joff's wife's life would have to be interviewed. And that included Joff himself. Even now two of Ian Roper's team were making discreet inquiries as to his whereabouts during the past three days. Deep down Joff must have know that but Mike Thorne was not going to state the obvious.

'Go down to the canteen and get something to eat. Or at least some strong black coffee,' he added, spotting the almost imperceptible shake of the head. Of course it would be impossible to eat. But down there would be other officers, someone who would speak to him, someone who might possibly break through the barrier PC Grant had thrown up around himself. And hopefully it would be someone in uniform who knew him well enough to feel able to intrude.

Mike Thorne sank back into his swivel chair which creaked

29

beneath his weight. He loosened his collar, fanned himself with the papers in front of him and began to reread the initial reports which had been sent to him regarding Jassy Grant's murder.

On paper everything pointed towards Petesy French. The circumstantial evidence was almost too good to be true. He couldn't remember leaving the pub, he had the gun which had probably killed her, he was found in the vicinity of the house. But circumstantial evidence counted for zilch. Thorne tapped his teeth with his gold-plated fountain pen. 'And it bloody well isn't his MO either,' he muttered – which, as he knew, also didn't mean a thing. There was always a first time.

DS Markham strolled into the Black Horse in Saxborough Road. Several pairs of eyes watched him without appearing to. But Markham noticed, much as he noticed everything which took place around him. He ignored the eyes and ordered a pint of lager because the bitter they served was unspeakably bad. In the corner, diagonally over his left shoulder, sat Sam Jenkins, an informer, but not a totally reliable one. He was apt to get things muddled. He had once alerted Markham to a job which had been set up by some locals and involved a substantial quantity of antiques. Jenkins had been correct in almost every detail. Except the address. As they had staked out a detached house on one side of Rickenham, the robbery had taken place on the other. This was always one of the dangers in using men like Sam Jenkins. If the villains learned who they were, and assuming they left them in one piece, they could use them for their own ends by feeding them misinformation which made the police look like idiots.

Markham turned slightly, casually altering his stance so that he was side-on to the bar. He sipped his drink and glanced at Jenkins over the rim of his glass. Jenkins looked down at his feet; he had nothing for the sergeant. They had several pre-arranged signals which were changed from time to time, just as their designated but isolated meeting points were used in rotation.

Tonight it was Markham's turn to make a sign. The Chief had arranged for two officers to speak to the landlord and get a list of all the customers who used the pub from the time French had entered until he had left. That was how it should be. Routine. Checking every word of French's statement and hopefully finding out what time he did leave and with whom, if anybody. But Markham's way was in through the back door. People like Jenkins would tell him things the landlord might conveniently forget rather than upset his regulars or have to admit that he had opened his doors early.

Markham walked past Jenkins's table without hesitation. He appeared to be deep in thought as he headed for the Gents. On his way back he glanced at his wrist-watch. Jenkins was good; his demeanour did not alter even fractionally as he continued sucking on a thin cigarette until it had burned down to his fingertips.

Markham leaned on the bar, his back to the room, and exchanged a few comments with a man on his right who was discussing a cricket match. Markham neither knew anything nor cared about the game, or any other sport, but, much as he hated it, he had to appear sociable when he was in the Black Horse. Some of the customers must be aware of who he was but he always acted as if the pub was simply his regular despite it being such a dump.

The new regime at the Prince William, or the Pink Elephant as it was now called, had done him a favour. When the clientele departed to fresh pastures, so did Markham. It made his case seem more genuine. He knew that Jenkins had received the signal. Markham's frown and pursed lips on the way to the toilets meant he wanted a meet. The glance at his watch on the way back meant in one hour's time. He ordered a second pint and tried to show interest in silly mid-offs, spin bowlers and maiden overs.

*

Petesy French lay on the bunk in his cell very much aware of the odours of his own body. They had taken away all he had stood up in but his landlady had been asked to bring in a change of clothes. None of that bothered him. His hangover did. Had he not been permitted to sleep for two hours it would not have been so bad. True, he would not be feeling great now but he would have gradually started to sober up. To have the process so rudely interrupted was more than he could bear. But how come he had such a bad one in the first place? He drank almost every day of his life and he hardly ever touched shorts. The cider in the Black Horse certainly had a kick to it but he couldn't remember drinking that much.

He had not been charged, not with the murder of the policeman's wife, his brain had registered that much, but he suspected it wouldn't be long. The other trivial matters didn't count.

Lying down, he remained rigid as he tried to get the metal grille shielding the light in the ceiling to swim properly into focus. It continued oscillating in much the same way as his thoughts. Slowly he stretched his arms, clasping his hands behind his head. He felt the roughness of the blanket which was not needed for warmth but for modesty.

With a great effort he made himself concentrate. All he had told them was true, he really did not recall leaving the Black Horse. 'You'll have to trust in our wonderful legal system,' he told himself cynically before he closed his eyes. If they left him alone all night he might have a chance of remembering in the morning. One thing he hoped would come back to him was where he had obtained the gun. That really puzzled him. He also hoped he might be allowed to have a shower.

At the precise moment that two officers were despatched to the home of Jasmine Grant's parents her body was being slid into one of the refrigerated drawers at the hospital mortuary where a post-mortem would be performed as soon as the requisite pathologist could be summoned.

The squad car entered the open iron gates of a large house in capacious grounds on the edge of Rickenham Green. There was no scrunching of gravel to warn the inhabitants of their arrival. The car moved smoothly up the pinkish surfaced drive in which minute particles of stone sparkled. Ahead was a three-storey building, the brickwork almost yellow as the evening sun dropped lower and its rays caressed the top two floors. Below, tall windows were opened on to a terrace where wrought iron furniture had recently been vacated.

PC Judy Robbins looked at her companion and raised her eyebrows. She and PC Michaels knew that the Goodwins were rich but this place spoke of old money, quiet money that had no use for ostentation. The simplicity of it all was deceiving. They were impressed.

The car rolled to a halt and they got out, shutting the doors quietly in deference to what they were about to do.

Voices could be heard from inside the open terrace windows, windows they would have to pass to reach the front door. It seemed rather ridiculous to have to do so but they could hardly tap casually on the glass as if they'd called in for a cup of tea. 'Come on,' Judy whispered, tucking her wayward white blouse into the tightly stretched waistband of her skirt. She coughed deliberately as they came in line with the occupied room.

'I think we've got visitors,' a refined female voice said.

Judy Robbins and Bob Michaels saw the shadowy figure come towards them. Erica Goodwin was framed in the double glass doors, her reflection visible in both sets of panes. She wore olive green culottes and a halter-neck top. Her feet were bare, the nails painted a pearly brown. Soft salt and pepper hair was wound in a casual coil on top of her head. 'Cliff! It's the police.' Erica took a hesitant step forwards. 'Excuse me. How rude I must have sounded. Only we didn't hear the car.'

A stoop-shouldered man appeared behind her. His limbs, protruding from white shorts and a polo shirt, were as tanned as those of his wife. He seemed less concerned to see them, his attitude suggesting that he thought they had probably come to warn him of a spate of burglaries. It was PC Michaels who broke the silence, clearing his throat nervously before he did so. How hard it was going to be to break the news to this couple who, minutes before, had been reading and enjoying a pre-dinner drink. Two glasses holding melting ice and a couple of paperbacks were on the table. 'Mr and Mrs Goodwin?'

'Yes?' Cliff put a protective arm around his wife's shoulders. He stood straighter, more tense, alerted by the serious tone of the constable.

'Would you like to sit down?' This from Judy Robbins, who was aware that those words alone would help to prepare them for what was to come. The Goodwins seemed not to know whether they should. Judy indicated the chairs and followed them to the table. Then she took over. 'I'm really sorry, there's no easy way to say this.' She paused to let her words sink in. 'There's been an incident which involved your daughter. She's been shot.'

'Shot?' Erica started to get out of her seat but her husband's hand restrained her.

Judy nodded. 'She's dead, Mrs Goodwin.' It was over. She had said it. How badly – how abruptly – but there never was an easy or better way.

'Flora? Our Flora?' Erica's eyes widened in horror and disbelief before she shook her head. 'No, she can't be.'

Christ, Judy thought. How careless she had been. She had known there were two daughters, it was logical for the parents to think that harm had come to the one in London, the one they saw less of.

'No, not Flora. Jasmine.' PC Michaels, guessing how Judy was feeling, stepped in to save her embarrassment.

'Jasmine?' Cliff repeated. He was as confused as his wife. The full implications had not hit them yet.

Judy and Bob had seen it before. The interrogative repetition of single phrases was one of the various reactions to initial disbelief. It was as if the speech area of the brain was being sparing with words because all the other areas were marshalling their forces to interpret the messages they did not want to receive.

'Oh, God.' Jasmine's father stared into the distance, across the grass and towards a clump of trees. His wife did not move. For a whole minute they were like four waxworks, their positions a contrivance of normality.

Judy swallowed, feeling superfluous as Cliff Goodwin reached across the table and took Erica's hand without looking at her. It was a natural gesture which showed how close they were. But Judy's duties were not yet over. Explanations were called for, the hows and the whens and the procedure which would be followed. The Goodwins must be told what to expect. There was also the task of informing other relatives if they did not wish to do so themselves. Another priority was to ensure the Goodwins had some support, either in the form of the police or someone of their own choice. 'Is there anyone else in the house, Mrs Goodwin?'

Erica shook her head. 'No. Mrs Maddern went an hour ago. She left us a light supper, some dips and things. She's very innovative with dips. We were going to eat out here. Oh, Cliff, tell me it isn't true.' The babble of words had released the lock on her mind's refusal to accept the unacceptable.

Cliff Goodwin rose and half lifted his wife from her seat. Enveloping her in his arms he softly shushed her, rocking her slightly as he held her. She sobbed quietly into his shoulder. Judy and Bob could only watch and wait.

'How did it happen? Was it a bank raid or something?' Cliff finally asked.

'No. She was at home. We believe she surprised an intruder.'

'I see.'

Erica released her grip on her husband's neck and pulled a tissue from the pocket of her culottes. In unison they sat down again. For the time being the parents of the murdered girl would only be interested in the facts. They would need to go through every detail, probably more than once, until they were finally able to grieve.

Superintendent Thorne had offered to go with Joff Grant to identify his wife's body but the offer had been refused. Thorne realised he might find it embarrassing to have a senior officer witness his anguish and left it at that.

Joff did go down to the canteen but only because he could think of nowhere else to go. It was some minutes before anyone spoke to him. Crime and injury and death were all part of the job but it was different when a colleague was involved. It was Sergeant William Baker who made the first move. He took his tea over to the table where Joff sat with his head bowed. 'I'll come to the ID with you,' he said simply and in a voice which did not allow for argument.

Joff nodded but did not speak. Bill Baker excused himself then went to the phone on the wall in the corner where he covered himself for the next couple of hours. He had heard that the body had been received at the mortuary and, although the chain of evidence had been adhered to and there was strictly no need for Joff to make a formal identification, William Baker knew that in the same position he, too, would have wanted to. Unfortunately for Joff there would be no prettying up of his wife's body. It could not be touched before the post-mortem examination.

It was a harrowing experience for both men. Bill Baker could not believe that what they were seeing was the remains of the lovely Jassy Grant and he didn't know how Joff was able to cope with it. But there was no doubt it was her. As they left the room Joff stumbled and grasped the door to steady himself.

'You're coming home with me,' was all Bill said, all he could say because he was so affected himself. He rang the station and said he was taking Joff back to his house where his wife would keep an eye on him until Bill came off duty.

36

Mrs Baker got the spare room ready and extra food out of the freezer but she had no idea what to say to her unexpected guest, no way of really helping him. All she could do was offer the basic comforts of food and drink and somewhere for him to sleep. She left Joff in the sitting-room whilst she prepared a meal but looked around the door every so often to ask if he wanted tea or coffee or a drink. On each occasion his position hadn't altered and the only answer she received was a shake of the head.

3

'Is he straight?' Richard Fry lifted a heavy cut glass tumbler to his lips. It contained a large measure of vintage brandy. He felt completely out of place but the first sip helped to settle him. He was driving, it would be his only drink, it would have to last.

His colleague, Oliver Bilton-Jones, arched an eyebrow and grinned as he held his own glass up to the light and examined its contents with pleasure.

'Well, you know what I mean,' Fry continued, aware that he had made himself appear foolish.

'Quite. And the answer is yes. He really has no other choice, you see.' Bilton-Jones was beginning to think it had been a mistake bringing Fry to the Elms. His own membership was not in any danger, he put too much money their way via the bar and the restaurant and in green fees. His guest's presence would not be challenged, Fry had been signed in, but he would not be introduced to anyone. To give Fry credit, he had adhered to his instructions, dressing appropriately for the occasion and making no attempt to establish eye contact with other members, let alone speak to them. Oliver Bilton-Jones had needed somewhere private where they could discuss certain matters. He had learned long ago that public places were far better venues than back streets or parked cars in country lanes where conversations might not be overheard but your presence would almost certainly be noticed. Far more respectable, and innocent, to take a fellow villain to the Elms Golf and Country Club. Not that Bilton-Jones considered himself to be a villain, he was more of a manipulator.

He was no ex-public schoolboy, bred and trained to mix in any circle, but had attended a state school; only through close observation and an inordinate amount of cunning had he acquired the mannerisms and tone of voice which indicated his education had been paid for. Bilton-Jones was now equally at home in any company.

The evening was still and sultry with the promise of thunder although none had been forecast. Four pairs of french windows were opened on to the terrace where groups of people talked quietly and sipped drinks as their ice melted and the thin slivers clinked against the sides of their glasses. Some of the members had showered and changed for dinner, others still wore their golfing clothes. Pastel polo shirts were much in evidence. Gnats flitted annoyingly around their heads and a moth surprised itself by entering the clubhouse after spending several minutes battering itself against a pane of glass in one of the doors.

Bilton-Jones noted it all, just as he noted everything in the room as he surveyed it quickly but expertly through the bottom of his upended glass. Faces were distorted but he knew them all, by sight or by reputation if not personally. None was as fully acquainted with him or his business deals. There was the usual group of five: estate agents and mortgage brokers who had fought hard to get into the club. Its membership was limited and there was a long waiting list. In a corner were the Eatons, a foolish pair: the husband a braggart when it came to money and his over-dressed blonde wife who had yet to realise that her charms had faded. She was having an affair with one of the estate agents but they were pointedly ignoring one another in the manner of the guilty.

Bilton-Jones knew this and had known it for some time. All knowledge was useful. In the corner of the bar, perched on a stool, elbows on the counter, was the badly dressed James Harris: Harris in his practice, the Doc in his capacity as one of the police surgeons attached to Rickenham Green headquarters. Despite his seemingly endless ambition to relieve the club of every drop of single malt whisky, the Doc was well liked and much respected as an old-fashioned GP. In his case the term 'old-fashioned' held no derogatory undertones; he was a man with a reputation for being able to listen and make a diagnosis without sending every second patient off to a specialist. His wife, his second wife, Shirley, would come and collect him later or he would take a taxi. Bilton-Jones was aware that the Doc's days of driving himself home at night were long over. There was nothing to be gained there. After discovering his tenuous connection with the police he had sounded the man out. Without knowing it, Doc Harris had been judged and found to be genuinely straight.

Richard Fry was finding difficulty in not staring at his fellow drinkers. There was money in the room, that much was obvious, and he wanted some of it. He wanted to be able to dress like Oliver, convinced that being able to do so would imbue him with confidence. But money wouldn't buy the height and broadness or the clear-cut features of the older man. Oliver Bilton-Jones was handsome and he had a knack of saying just the right thing to put people at ease. That was probably why he was able to con them.

Fry was known as the Ferret, which was an apt enough description of his thin face with its long pointed nose and eyes set too closely together; none of which he could help. Employed variously as a driver, a go-between and general dogsbody, he was not used to being in such opulent surroundings although all around him people were just as relaxed as if they were in their own homes. One day, he thought to himself, one day I shall be one of them. All he had to do was to stick with Bilton-Jones for a little longer.

'Ah, yes. Same again, please, Charles.' Bilton-Jones slid his glass towards the bar steward and threw down a twenty-pound note. Two or three people coming in from the terrace for dinner greeted him before going through to the dining-room. 'We'll get the second half next week,' he told Fry in a normal voice, quite casually, knowing that whispers drew attention. 'Meanwhile we carry on as before. No hiding away, no avoiding the usual places. Is that clear?'

Fry nodded, wishing he could have another drink. What Oliver said made sense, that was probably why he had done so well for himself. But the brandy, which he wasn't used to, had brought his resentment to the surface. Bilton-Jones, in his tailor-made trousers and Italian short-sleeved shirt, was over-weight rather than broad, he decided. An inch or so of soft flesh rested on the leather belt. And it was insulting not to be allowed to buy a drink. He could afford to, especially here where, contrary to what he had imagined, the bar tarriff was cheaper than the pubs of the town. Was it because he spoke with the local Suffolk accent that Bilton-Jones had said he wasn't to offer? Life wasn't fair. But he would bide his time. Every dog has its day, he told himself.

'What do you know about the Howard lad?'

'Mark Howard?' Fry was cautious. Bilton-Jones knew they were friends, he was obviously after something. 'He's OK. Why?'

'Just wondered. Looking for work, is he?'

'He might be.'

'Find out, would you?'

Before Richard Fry could answer, his companion began talking to someone on his left. Cut to the quick at this cavalier treatment he fumed silently until it was time to leave.

In the early hours of Thursday morning, half an hour before the alarm was set to go off, DCI Roper opened his eyes and wondered why he was awake. Not one to come around quickly and spring out of bed as Moira was able to do, he knew it was work which was on his mind. Jassy Grant, to be specific, and he had to attend the post-mortem.

His mind was unable to perform the mental acrobatics of which some others of his rank were capable, but not because he was slow or stupid or too old for the job. The explanation lay in his training. He had been taught to approach every problem logically, systematically and methodically. Boring it might be, but in the end it got results. Mostly. It was all very well knowing the answers in advance but they had to fit the questions. The Crown Prosecution Service needed proof, not ideas.

And that was what had woken him. Yesterday afternoon he had 'known' that Petesy French was guilty, last night he had been doubtful, and sometime during the night he had come to wonder how he could have been so certain.

Ian sighed, swung his feet to the floor and turned off the alarm before it shrilled rudely. Downstairs sunlight filled the kitchen but as he made tea he saw the whitening sky and knew it would be another unbearable day. The back door was open. Worse than being bright and hot, it was overcast and muggy with the promise of humidity which would build up under cloud cover.

The floorboards overhead creaked as Moira made her way to the bathroom. He hoped he had not disturbed her. He shaved at the kitchen sink, a habit left over from the days when he had worked early shifts and Mark was a baby and the house where they lived had had noisy bathroom plumbing. By the time he had finished Moira appeared, showered and dressed. 'It's all right, I was too hot to sleep,' she said.

She was now the personal assistant to the managing director of the garage on Saxborough Road which sold cars costing the equivalent of a two-up, two-down cottage in Station Road. Ian felt a mixture of resentment and envy towards those who could afford one of them.

Moira kissed him absentmindedly. 'I'll be late tonight. I'm having a drink with Denis and John then I'm going to see

41

Lucy. She thinks she'll be home today. If not, I'll go to the hospital.'

Ian nodded. 'I expect I'll be late, too.' He handed Moira a mug of tea.

Ten minutes later he left the house. A lorry was blocking the road between the two lines of parked cars. It was a removal van. Someone must have had an early start. He had not realised that the house with the sold sign was already empty. Ian cursed, changed gear and, with one arm slung over the back of the passenger seat, reversed to the end of Belmont Terrace. It was not an auspicious start to the day.

As soon as he arrived at work he checked that DC Alan Campbell had been pulled off the ABH cases and reinstated in his own team. He had, and DC Hanson had taken over from him. In his office he made a list of what he would like to achieve that day, once he had heard what DS Markham (unofficially) and DC Gibbons (officially) had found out. Petesy French might or might not be in the clear; either way they must widen the circle of their inquiries.

They now knew that Joff had booked an Apex ticket for his trip and had travelled on the relevant trains, arriving at the resort on Saturday and spending his time in the presence of plenty of witnesses.

According to the calendar on the kitchen wall Jasmine had planned to see Sally Foster during Joff's absence. The 1991 diary kept next to the telephone contained only names, addresses and numbers. There were many crossings out where people had moved and the leather cover was worn and faded.

Jassy didn't work, unusual now for someone who had no children and who was young and, presumably, healthy. Which reminded Ian – the post-mortem was due to take place in half an hour and he had better hurry. Leaving a message for Markham to say he was to take charge of the briefing if Ian had not returned in time, he collected DC Alan Campbell who had arrived ahead of him and they left the building, stepping out of the air-conditioning into the sticky heat.

Ian hated the macabre mortuary and all that went on within it. As a precaution he had not eaten breakfast. DC Campbell had no such qualms. Stick insect thin, his pale blue eyes almost colourless and everything about him so typically Scottish, he greeted the Chief with a smile and a paper bag which was spotted with grease.

They got into the back of their car as their allocated driver started the engine.

'Bit of a rush this morning, sir. Want one? They're yesterday's but they're all right,' Alan explained as he extracted a jam doughnut from the bag, having first offered it to Ian who had shaken his head vehemently. By the time they reached the hospital Alan had eaten both.

There was a respectful silence when the see-through body-bag was removed from the corpse. Ian swallowed hard as he watched Campbell wipe some grains of sugar from his chin and lick his fingers.

The grisly scene was endured but the pathologist had not been able to add much to what they already knew. Jasmine Grant, née Goodwin, had died from gunshot wounds. She was healthy and neither pregnant nor menstruating at the time of her death. No sexual intercourse had recently taken place and her last, small, meal had been eaten several hours before she was killed.

During the drive back to the station Alan Campbell consumed a Kit-Kat. It had been in his pocket overnight and was misshapen. Most of the chocolate coating was stuck to the silver paper which, to Ian's disgust, he licked before he screwed it into a tiny ball and stuffed it into the ashtray beside him.

Ian was thinking about the ABHs. It was Campbell who had pointed out that the apparently motiveless attacks were aimed at businessmen. There had also been a number of shop windows smashed but that was par for the course at weekends. Still, that was now Hanson's worry.

'There's someone waiting to see you. Flora Goodwin,' Ian was informed upon his return. 'She wants to speak to who-ever's in charge.'

'Don't they all,' Ian muttered. 'OK, get her down to one of the interview rooms.' The older Goodwin sister lived in London. She must have travelled up last night or set off in the early hours.

Flora Goodwin had come of her own accord and had been described as assertive. A few minutes alone in one of those unwelcoming rooms usually quelled bluster and bullshit.

Ian gave it ten minutes before joining her. He was taken aback at the young woman sitting calmly at the table. She was smoking a cigarette and tapping ash on the floor. As sisters, no two females could have been less alike. Flora was as slender as Jassy but did not possess the same curves. Her chin-length bob and straight fringe looked as if each individual hair had been measured before it was cut. It shone unbelievably even though it was too black to be her natural colour. Her skin was pale and her lipstick bright. 'Good morning, Miss Goodwin. I'm Chief Inspector Roper.' For some reason he got the impression that condolences would be a waste of time. 'Was there a specific reason you wanted to see me?'

'I imagined it might be the other way around.'

Taken aback by the woman's cold manner Ian pulled out a chair and sat down, giving himself a few seconds to decide how to deal with her. 'We have arrested someone, if that is what you are referring to.'

Flora Goodwin seemed surprised. Her brows arched a little. 'Already? In that case . . .' She stood and picked up her handbag which was lying on the table. It was envelope-style in soft ochre leather and matched her shoes. Both toned with her tan linen suit. She had certainly dressed for the occasion. 'Do my parents know of the arrest?'

It was an odd question but presumably Judy Robbins or Bob Michaels would have told them. He avoided an answer. 'Whilst you're here, Miss Goodwin, could you spare me a few more minutes?' She sat down again. 'We need to know as much as possible about your sister. In cases such as this it always helps.'

'I can't see how, not if you've already got the man. Ah, I see. You're not sure if it is him.'

It was an astute observation. 'What was she like?'

Flora shrugged. 'We didn't know each other that well as adults. Once I moved we grew apart. We were very different, you see. Jassy was always more compliant. I think she was my parents' favourite.

'They wanted us both to spend a year abroad once we'd finished school. Can you imagine it? I thought that sort of thing went out with the ark. I refused to go. I got a job in London and have worked my way up the ladder. That year abroad would have been wasted on me.'

'What is it you do, Miss Goodwin?'

Her eyes narrowed as if he had vaguely offended her by not knowing. 'I'm a beauty editor on a magazine. I live and work in London, it's the only place to be. Jassy's never worked. She trolled off to Paris and Switzerland like a good girl. Not long after she got back she met Joff at a party and they were married within six months.' The way she spoke implied that she considered her sister had wasted the short life she had had.

'Did you know any of her friends?'

'No. And I would have thought that with Joff being a policeman you would know more about them than I.'

Ian refused to be rattled. 'Joff's devastated. He's taking it very badly.'

'That's hardly surprising. But no doubt he'll miss the lifestyle.'

Ian stood. It was an unkind remark, the woman was a bitch and he did not like her. She had shown no compassion for Joff and seemed completely unconcerned that her sister had been murdered. 'Well, I won't keep you any longer. I'm sure your parents need you.'

'Yes. I'm on my way there. I wanted to be able to give

them some good news. But if they already know ...' She shrugged again. It was an offhand gesture but Ian wondered if she had hoped to be the one to tell them the police had arrested someone and therefore gain something in her parents' eyes.

He showed her to the end of the corridor then asked a WPC to escort her to the main entrance.

'Barry? I wasn't expecting to see you today.' DS Swan had appeared just as Ian was about to send for Markham. 'Everything all right?'

'Oh, fine. I can't pick up Lucy and the baby until four thirty. I thought I'd call in and catch up a bit. So Petesy French has hit the big time.' Barry waited, watching Ian's face. 'You don't think it was French?'

'It's just too sodding neat.'

'Who was the bimbo?'

'The victim's sister. You'd need an ice pick to crack her hard casing.' And Flora had obliquely expressed jealousy of Jassy. He knew he was clutching at straws. There was no way a woman like that would pass the time of day with Petesy French, let alone get near enough to plant a gun on him. She had a career, one which obviously paid well: money would not have been the motive. And with that thought he realised that the idea of the gun having been planted had been in his subconscious for some time. It would not have been an impossible task because French had been in a drunken stupor when he was picked up.

Before Barry could offer any sort of opinion Markham banged on the door. As he entered he glanced at Barry but did not speak to him. 'Sir, what we've got doesn't come to much more than a definite leaving time from the pub. As he said, French got a paper, etcetera, went home, then placed his bet. From the bookie's he went straight to the Black Horse where he became involved in a session, although no one can remember him drinking more than usual. According to the witnesses, including my informant, French left there at twelve thirty or thirty-five. Alone. They remember because he was

46

staggering and crashed into a table and dropped his hold-all. He claimed to be going to the launderette. The nearest one's in Saxborough Road, but in the opposite direction to the one he must have taken to be found where he was at a few minutes past one.'

It didn't look too good for French. He had had enough time to get to the Grants' house, shoot Jassy and make it back to where he was found. 'Sergeant, would you mind checking the details of how he was found?'

'A patrol car—'

Ian held up a hand. 'Yes, I know that. But why? Was it just passing or did someone call for them?'

'I'll find out.'

It should have been picked up before. A mistake had been made. French had been brought in on a minor charge, the details of how or why he had been found had seemed irrelevant at the time. If someone had rung to make a complaint it could mean several things, not least of which was that there was a witness who had seen him after he left the Black Horse and who may have noticed where he was coming from before he collapsed. But a more sinister explanation was that somebody wanted him found, and found with the gun in his possession. It was not over yet by a long way.

Markham had been disappointed in Sam Jenkins, who knew no more than the other customers, yet something was amiss. Markham had sensed it. He had no idea what was going on at the Black Horse or even if it was connected with the killing but there were underlying currents he didn't understand.

He knew Tony Peak, the landlord, reasonably well. He had no form, which did not mean the same applied to all his clientele, but that was no reason to withhold his licence. He also knew that certain of these customers could get a drink before 11 a.m. And that occasionally there was a 'lock-in' after hours. A raid would have served no purpose, the drinkers would simply go elsewhere for the extra service, possibly scattering to different pubs. As long as there was no trouble it was better to have them all under one roof where

Markham and his informants could keep an eye on them. He did not think that Tony Peak was stupid enough to have become involved in something criminal but it was always a possibility. The man lived on the premises and there was plenty of room upstairs to store property that had been parted from its rightful owner.

No, Tony did not come across as stupid and he was, in a strange way, a likeable man. But Markham was uneasy. He decided to follow his instincts and dig a little deeper. All this went through his mind before he was out of the door.

Barry Swan made no attempt to do any work. He sat on the edge of Ian's desk, one leg swinging, his arms folded. 'Why not French?'

Ian scowled. Sergeant Swan, no, Inspector Swan had no business being so happy. He turned to open the window, negating the effects of the air-conditioning but he wanted a cigarette. He turned to Barry, who was wearing trousers and a short-sleeved shirt. He had never known him to wear jeans. The heat slowly invaded the room and caused a film of sweat to shine on Ian's brow. A storm was needed, and rain, but he hoped the storm would not occur within the walls of Rickenham Green headquarters if they got it all wrong. He was barely listening as Barry recounted the embarrassing incident at the Taj Mahal. He was too busy thinking about motives. The only plausible one was the one they had already, that Petesy French had made the most of an opportunity. Drunk and therefore possibly braver than he was wont to be, he had found an unlocked door and entered the premises but was interrupted before he had time to nick anything. He had a gun, and people who carry guns will, when cornered, use them, even if this was not their original intention.

Their prisoner had been fed and watered at the required intervals. The custody officer had reported that French had hardly stirred during the night and was now clean and tidy and totally sober. He was making noises, demanding to see a solicitor and the person responsible for banging him up. The

48

former request had already been granted, the latter was about to be.

'I'm off now. Things to do,' Barry said, levering himself off the desk, disappointed that Ian was not in the mood to share his enthusiasm for fatherhood. Conversely, he was sorry not to be part of the team. For once he was an outsider whilst other men and women strove to prove or disprove what they believed had taken place the previous day.

Ian picked up the phone and asked DC Brenda Gibbons to accompany him. Too much testosterone in one room would probably not further their case against Petesy French but a little femininity might.

'When we've finished, pay a visit to the parents. The other daughter's there now. Flora Goodwin.'

Brenda nodded and followed Ian into the interview room where French was already seated at the table under the careful watch of his guard. Beside him sat Peter Jones, one of the duty solicitors, who would already have advised him how to answer the questions. Ian did not know Jones very well so could not guess at his methods accurately. He had not been qualified long and he was a new addition to the duty rota.

Petesy looked up and took in Brenda's every detail with one sweeping glance. Approval showed in his face. 'Now that's what I call a copper,' he said, ignoring the warning look from Jones.

It was Brenda who set up the tape and went through the introductory procedures, so familiar they were boring. Ian nodded: she was to take the initiative.

'Mr French, yesterday afternoon you were apprehended at the end of Maple Drive. At the time you had consumed a considerable amount of alcohol.'

'Yeah. I was pissed.'

Jones raised his eyes to the ceiling and sat back, folding his arms. The body language suggested that his new client was nothing to do with him.

'In your possession was a firearm for which you do not hold a licence, a firearm which we now know was used to kill Jasmine Grant.' It had been confirmed although it was no surprise to anyone.

Petesy chewed his lip. His brief had clearly outlined his predicament and had advised him to say nothing. 'Not much I can say when I don't remember a bloody thing,' he had retorted less than an hour previously, only to be told very firmly that, if he did speak, whatever he said must not be a repetition of that statement.

'Where did you get the gun?'

Without consulting Jones, who was getting on his nerves, French answered, 'I don't know and that's God's honest truth. I went out for a paper—'

'You told us all that yesterday.'

'Did I?' He wondered what else he might have said. But they'd have to let him read any statement if he'd made one.

'We want to know what happened after you left the Black Horse.'

'I didn't have any gun on me when I left my digs. All I had was my washing. I was going to put my bet on, have a couple of drinks then get a sandwich and a cup of tea in the place over the road from the launderette while the washing was doing.'

'The Fast Clean launderette?'

'Yes. Just down from the pub.'

'But you didn't do your washing and you had no intention of doing so. You went in the opposite direction.' Brenda knew that the Chief approved of her handling of the suspect; had he not done so he would have interrupted by now.

'Do you know, I can sort of recall going the other way, but damn me if I know why I changed my mind.'

Jones groaned. His client might as well sign a confession statement. He tapped Petesy on the arm, a pre-arranged signal which was supposed to shut him up. 'I think my client would like a break for a consultation.'

'No, I fucking well wouldn't.' He was on his feet. 'What

I'd like is to know how I came by that gun. You know my form, Mr Roper, you know I never go tooled up.'

Jones sat back, red-faced, and wondering what he was doing there.

'Please calm down, Mr French. Losing your temper won't help.' Brenda gave him a reassuring smile. She had not stirred during the outburst. She had noticed the man's agitation increasing and had been prepared for it. Unfortunately she believed him. Petesy French was not lying when he said he had no idea of his movements yesterday afternoon. If he stuck to his story about the gun there was no way they could prove anything different. She persevered. 'Where did you get the gun?' Occasionally a question repeated to the point of obsession could get a result. But not this time.

Petesy rubbed his head and gave an exaggerated sigh. 'Look, I keep telling you, I don't know. It isn't mine. I've never seen it before. You say you found it on me, so I suppose I have to believe you. Hell, you could've put it there for all I know.' He was still unable to recall leaving the Black Horse although vague memories stirred at the back of his mind. He hoped that if they ever rose to the surface they would not prove him to be guilty. Guns terrified him and he was sure that no matter how drunk he had been he would not have had one in his possession, let alone have fired it, supposing he knew how to. On the other hand, he had never been that drunk before.

'Tell us what you can remember about the time you spent in the Black Horse. Tell us who you were with.' Brenda spoke quietly as she brushed back a tendril of hair. She might have been encouraging a small child in some difficult task.

'Jesus! Again? I chatted to Tony. Like I said, he's the guv'nor. Then some of the lads came in and we had a few drinks.' He ran through a handful of names. 'Next thing is, I fell over in the bog.' He lifted an arm and displayed a slightly swollen elbow with a bruise starting to form. 'Don't worry, I shan't be making a complaint of police brutality.' His gap-toothed grin at his feeble joke only got a response from Jones, who leaned forward and literally put his head in his hands as he shook it in despair.

Petesy French's memory took him no further than the Gents in the Black Horse. DC Gibbons thought it would have been more profitable to have spent the time on Aldeburgh beach.

'What?' DCI Ian Roper stared at Markham. The call had been logged at 13.02 the previous day. A man living in Maple Drive had rung in to complain that a drunk was shouting and swearing and waving about in the road. He gave his name as David Wright, his address as number four. 'Get someone round to see him immediately.'

'There's no point, sir. I've checked. The couple who live at number four are called Wilson. Their children have left home and they're both out at work all day. Neither of them claims to have made the call. He's a dentist and she's a part-time secretary at Rickenham General. Mrs Wilson got home around three thirty, her husband a little after seven. No one by the name of Wright lives in Maple Drive.'

In the ensuing silence they were both thinking the same thing. The few residents who had been at home had seen no one behaving in the manner described. Someone had wanted Petesy French to be found.

'One and two squads have completed door-to-door, get number three moving on follow-up, but make sure they're aware of this call, make sure they don't miss a single thing. I don't want another slip-up.' Ian paused. He leaned back against his desk and crossed his legs at the ankles. His chin was in the palm of one hand, his elbow resting in the other hand. 'There's always the possibility that someone in the road did ring but gave a false name because they didn't want to be involved or gain a reputation as a trouble-maker. Perhaps they even feared repercussions. Find out. I want to know.'

Markham's gait was deceiving. He seemed to stroll out of the room yet he covered a lot of ground quickly.

'If the gun was planted, what then?' Ian asked the sheet of glass as he turned to look out over the street. Women in summer dresses and short skirts paraded along the pavements. He swung the locking catch and opened the window, despite admonishments from those concerned with the budget not to do so. The scent of roses surprised him. Now in full bloom in the raised flower beds at the entrance, the short-stemmed varieties were at their best. Only a few petals lay on the dry soil. Ian's lips twitched. Guns and Roses. Mark used to drive him mad playing music by a group of that name. Band, he reminded himself; the word 'group' dated him. Heavy metal, whatever that meant. But the gun wasn't heavy enough to make Petesy wonder what was in with his washing, if he was capable of noticing anything, that is. And if the gun was planted, what reason did anyone have to kill Jasmine Grant? Ian chewed a loose piece of skin at the side of his thumb, regretting it instantly as he drew blood. He ran a hand through his thick brown hair. It was a gesture of desperation. It would be another long day. He needed to read the results of the house-to-house inquiries and he wanted everyone even vaguely connected with firearms offences to be interviewed. It suddenly semed important to find out where the Heckler & Koch came from. Someone out there knew, or at least knew where such a weapon could be obtained in this part of the country.

'And now for the long haul,' Ian muttered, knowing that each and every person who had touched Jasmine Grant's life would need to be spoken with. The innocence of Petesy French, at least in this instance, seemed more likely with every passing hour. Ian was impatient to receive the lists of Jassy's connections. Names had already been taken from letters and documents in the house as well as from the diary kept by the telephone but her family had also agreed to help, as had Joff himself although Ian doubted his ability to perform such a task with any accuracy at the moment.

He cursed Barry Swan, with whom he would dearly have loved to discuss the case. He would have to get used to the fact that Barry was leaving despite his having tried to persuade him not to. Lucy was in favour of it too. He stood no chance, not with a woman on the other side.

There had been talk of moving DC Gibbons one step up the ladder. She, too, had been going to take exams but Ian had spoken to her, told her that she wasn't ready yet, that even if she passed he would not recommend her for a post as sergeant.

'I will be next time,' she had answered, controlling her anger, holding back comments about sexism because she knew that as far as the Chief was concerned they would be unfounded; unfounded for the very reason that she suspected he *was* sexist and therefore went out of his way to prove otherwise.

Ian had silently congratulated her. Many females would have made such a comment even knowing it was untrue.

4

Avril Baker was not the sort of wife a stranger would imagine the sergeant to have married. William Baker was, and always had been, old before his years. Overweight, with greying hair brushed straight back from his forehead in a style very much out of date, he gave the impression of being comfortable in his self-imposed role. But impressions are just that. For his size he was remarkably fit and he was well aware that he projected a 'safeness' that was extremely deceptive. He might look like a nice, placid copper but that was far from the truth. In fact, it was his wife who was the more placid of the two. Avril was taller than her husband but not by much and this did not prevent her wearing high heels when the occasion arose. Apart from her twenty-three-inch waist, in which she took pride, she was a modest woman, surprisingly so because she could turn heads far younger than her own shiny black-haired one. As a child and a young woman she had been plain and this had influenced her self-image. Emerging, in her mid-twenties, from the ugly duckling syndrome, she had never come to terms with the fact that now, in the last year of her thirties, she was a very attractive woman.

She stood in the kitchen of the two-up, two-down house she and Bill had shared for almost twenty-one years, during which time they had modernised and upgraded it. Bill Baker had an eye for such things. Both his home and his woman had become more beautiful as time progressed.

Avril was leaning against the electric cooker, the end of a spatula pressed to her lips. She wore jeans and a plain white T-shirt and her hair was held on the top of her head by a spring-toothed clip disguised by a chiffon flower. Shorts would have been more in keeping with the weather but it seemed somehow disrespectful with Joff Grant under her roof. Bacon was waiting in the fridge but she had not yet turned on the grill in case Joff was not up to eating. He had gone to bed at ten the previous night and she had not heard a sound since although she could not imagine he had had much sleep.

A creak overhead warned her that he was up. A few minutes later she heard the toilet flush and water draining from the immersion heater which had always been noisy. The bathroom walls had been retiled not long ago and there was new cork flooring which was warm underfoot. Avril knew it was irrelevant, that Joff wouldn't notice, but she was glad she'd cleaned the bathroom yesterday. It was small, as were all their rooms, but they had turned it back into the cottage-style dwelling it had originally been. 'God, what'll I say to him?' she whispered to the border collie in his basket as she bent down to stroke his head. Joff hadn't uttered more than a handful of words yesterday.

The kitchen door opened and Joff stood there, framed in the opening. His eyes were bleary but he had shaved, using one of Bill's disposable razors as he did not have one in the hold-all he had taken on his fishing trip. He was unnaturally pale and from where she stood Avril could see he was trembling. 'Would you like some breakfast?' Her grey eyes showed the compassion which she felt but she wished she was more adept at coping in moments like these.

'No, please, I don't want to put you to any trouble. I'll leave as soon as I've got somewhere to go.'

'There's no need for that, Joff, we've got a spare room, you may as well use it. I know it's a bit feminine, but it's yours for as long as you want it.' It had been their daughter's room but, like her mother, she had married young, at eighteen, and, following in the family tradition, had become pregnant imme- diately. Avril Baker was thrilled at the prospect of becoming a grandmother because, despite their efforts, she and Bill had had no more children.

'Well, in that case ... I wouldn't mind, actually.' Joff straightened his shoulders as if he had decided to be strong to face up to whatever lay ahead. He even managed a weak smile.

Avril chewed her lip. Wouldn't mind what? The room or breakfast? 'Two eggs?' she asked, trying to sound cheerful, knowing that she would have to join him at the table and make some pretence at conversation.

'Yes, please.'

She found it odd that he had any appetite although he had hardly touched the food she had prepared for him last night. 'The kettle's just boiled – tea or coffee?'

'Coffee, please.'

Joff sat down, squeezing himself into the chair between the table and the fitted cupboards behind him. His hair was as black as Avril's and, with his own good looks, they might have been related. He watched her narrow back as she set about cooking bacon and eggs.

'If they need to speak to you, you know, the police, you're welcome to the front room.' She was not sure if this was the most tactful thing to say but she had been married to a policeman long enough to know it was more than likely. 'I've got to go out later so just make yourself at home.' Redness crept into her face. She was making a right hash of trying to be tactful. She opened the back door but felt no cooler. How could Joff feel at home anywhere after what had happened? She decided it was safer to keep her mouth shut.

Only when the food was in front of him did Joff speak again. 'How could anyone do such a thing? And to Jassy of all people. Oh, God, what am I going to do, Avril?'

Avril's maternal feelings came to her rescue. She got up and held his head against her stomach as the tears flowed. 'They'll catch him. You know that better than anyone. It'll be all right, sometime in the future it'll be all right.' But they didn't always catch them and Joff knew that better than anyone.

He shook his head. 'But it won't bring her back.' His face was screwed up with emotion but Avril saw that he would not allow himself to cry again in front of her. She imagined that something in him had died too.

Gratified to see his empty plate she offered him more coffee. He looked a little better for the food.

'You've got a nice little place here,' he commented as she handed him his refilled cup.

Avril glanced around the kitchen. Yes, it was nice. She and Bill had worked hard to make it so, yet it was nowhere near the league she had heard Joff's house was in. Under the circumstances she thought it an odd thing to say. It must appear cramped compared with what he was used to and she was surprised he had noticed at all. Perhaps, like herself, he had no idea what to say but felt obliged to make conversation. She only worked part-time now, temping three days a week. For the past month she had been at the same place, typing and filing invoices and dealing with other bits of paperwork for a long distance haulage company. The work was dull and repetitive but it got her out of the house and earned her some extra money, and it was only another week before the new permanent girl started and she could move on. For once she was thankful to be going in. Impossible to imagine spending the rest of the day with Joff. It was a selfish thought but nonetheless true and she suspected that she was not the only one who would be grateful.

'Had enough?' She removed his plate and gestured to his coffee cup.

'I wouldn't mind another. I didn't sleep, it'll help keep me awake today,' he added hastily, noticing the look of surprise on her face. He turned away quickly, not wanting to see how attractive Bill's wife was, nor to have to wonder if Jassy would have still been so at that age. The telephone rang and saved them both from further embarrassment.

'It's Chief Inspector Roper. He wants to know if you're up to answering some questions.'

'Yes, of course.'

Avril put a hand on his shoulder as he started to get up. 'No, not now. He just asked me to ask you. If it's OK, someone'll come over later.'

Joff nodded, his mouth a grim line. It had to be done sometime or another: he knew they would have to check his whereabouts. But the thought of being interviewed by his colleagues was not a pleasant one.

The sun streamed in through the open door and window, creating two different-sized parallelograms of light on the quarry-tiled floor. The threatened thunder had not come. Last night, for an hour or so, the humidity had increased and the sky had darkened so that it seemed inevitable, but not even a few spots of rain had fallen to settle the dust and relieve the parched lawns and flowers from the drought. Had she not been going out to work Avril would have lazed in the garden in her bikini. With Joff here it would have been impossible. Her hours today were from eleven until four. Bill was on an early shift and would be home before her which would ease the burden on her somewhat.

Having cleared the table and washed up, she handed Joff the newspaper which they had delivered and asked if he wanted to sit outside. 'There're garden chairs in the shed, or you can use the lounger if you prefer. I've got to get ready for work now.'

58

Avril took her time and felt guilty for doing so but it was apparent Joff would rather be alone. When she came down there was no sign of him in the house. To her surprise she found him lying full length on the sun-lounger, his face held up to the heat of the sun. Beside him, on the yellowed lawn, lay the paper. 'I'm off now, Joff. Bill'll be home around three. Just help yourself to anything you fancy. There're some cold beers in the fridge.'

'Thanks, Avril. See you later.'

With a puzzled frown she re-entered the house, picked up her bag and left via the front door.

The news had travelled fast. On Thursday lunchtime the regulars at the Black Horse were subdued, especially those who had form: they knew that until the case was closed, if it ever was, there would be no peace for them. The murder of a policeman's wife meant trouble. They, the opposition, would want revenge – and where more likely to take it than on those who had already transgressed?

Tony Peak unnecessarily polished the glasses as he took them from the dishwasher. This sort of thing wasn't good for business. The police might be keeping an eye on the place, which meant his after hours trade would have to be temporarily halted. And after hours was where he made serious money. He supposed no publican was enthralled with having the police hanging around the place.

There was nothing official yet but they all knew that Petesy French had been taken in for questioning and had probably, by now, been arrested. French was not popular because he tended to impose himself on people and it was well known that he was incompetent, but he was one of their own. Not one of them believed he was a killer.

Mark Howard, one of the few who had time for Petesy, was pale-faced. They were of an age, both in their mid-twenties, both unemployed and with the same penchant for the horses. It was only a matter of time before the police came for him. He was known to hang around with Petesy and there was a recent occasion when they had found two cartons of blank video cassettes in his bed-sitting-room. They hadn't found the other two, which were in the loft of the house where he had a room, but he would have to ditch them now and cut his losses. One more court appearance and he'd go down, he knew that, and it wasn't worth it for a few quid.

Another round was ordered and Tony served it with a frown on his round, sweaty face which was mostly hidden under a thick beard with more grey in it than his hair.

Richard Fry walked in, on cue, in time to be included in the round. On Thursdays he and Oliver always had lunch in the Taj Mahal after a drink or two in the Black Horse; soft drinks for Fry, however. Their weeks had more or less a regular pattern and this week, more than ever, they intended to stick to it.

For the next hour the discussion centred around the murder. Tony Peak had had enough of it. Taking two pound coins from the till he went over to the juke-box and made some selections then he went back behind the bar and turned up the sound.

DC Potter sat to one side of the high hospital bed half reading a two-day-old newspaper which he had found on the chair, half watching the occupant of the bed. The other man in the side ward was still unconscious, drips and tubes protruding from various points of his body. One eye had disappeared beneath a mushy purple swelling where four tight black sutures held the skin together. It looked painful but David Sadiqi was not yet aware of his injuries.

Justin Potter had relieved a PC who had spent several boring hours waiting for the victim to open his eyes, or, at least, his one good eye. The doctor responsible for Sadiqi's treatment had informed him that the combination of the analgesic and hypnotic drugs the patient had been given was wearing off, that Mr Sadiqi was now in a shallow sleep. DC Potter hoped it didn't last too long. He hated hospitals.

Within fifteen minutes there was a low moan from the bed. Potter slung the newspaper on to the locker top and stood up. 'Mr Sadiqi?' he said quietly, hoping to get some information out of him before a nurse or the doctor returned. 'What did you say? I didn't hear you.' The injured man had mumbled something from between bruised lips but his teeth, very white against his brown skin, seemed to be intact.

Twice they were interrupted by medical staff who came to do their fifteen-minute checks. Nothing was said but both nurses gave little nods of satisfaction before recording their findings on the charts hanging over the bottom rail of the bed.

Speech was obviously painful but David Sadiqi managed to explain that he had been set upon a few minutes after closing up his off-licence and video rental shop the previous evening. It would have been ten fifteen or ten twenty by the time he had put the money in the safe, secured the window grilles and locked up. No, he didn't know the man, he hadn't even seen his face, and no, he hadn't been robbed and he didn't know anyone who bore him a grudge. Perhaps, he suggested timidly, it was because of the colour of his skin.

Potter didn't think so. There were still few Asians in Rickenham Green and they kept to themselves, running their small businesses. There were no gangs of youths to fight with white gangs and, as far as he knew, there had not been a racist attack in the town. But there had been other attacks. As Sadiqi's good eye slowly closed Potter knew he would get no more out of him for a while. He left the side ward and went to the sister's office and asked if he might use the phone. Reporting the little he had discovered, he was told to return to base.

Potter would add his meagre findings to those DC Campbell had come up with before he had been taken off the case. Hanson was in charge now – at least he had a sense of humour. These sort of crimes were escalating. Every local newspaper gave accounts of innocent people being attacked for no apparent reason, not even for the contents of their wallets or handbags. But three in less than a fortnight? There had been Dyfan Roberts who ran the London Hotel, a six-bedroomed place which catered for commercial businessmen during the week and offered weekend breaks from Friday to Sunday. It had taken over from the Station Arms which had now been pulled down to make way for development. The third victim, Tony Gregson, was the owner of a corner shop, unimaginatively named Convenience Store, which he had modernised in the way of all such premises; there was now a row of shelving down the middle and a trolley of baskets so that customers could help themselves and pay at the till. If these men had been carrying the takings it would have been a different matter. Potter's mind was working overtime as he drove back to the station. He knew exactly what he was going to do, unless Alan Campbell in his methodical manner had already asked Hanson to do it.

Sally Foster was still shaken. Yesterday, after finding Jassy on her own kitchen floor, her face and neck blown apart, what she had witnessed hardly seemed to register but with each passing hour it became more of a nightmare. Waiting for the police to arrive, she wished she had given them a full statement at the time because she did not know how she would be able to go through it all again. Her pleasant face was blotchy with crying and lack of sleep and her mid-brown hair, washed only yesterday morning, had turned lank. She pushed it behind her ears and smoothed down the denim skirt she was wearing. Her husband had rung her boss and told him the reason why she wouldn't be in. She worked in the town hall, on flexitime; yesterday she had used up hours owing to her and taken the day off to lie in the garden and start thinking about the next production the Drama Guild was going to perform. Ibsen, *Hedda Gabler*, an ambitious project but Sally believed they were ready for it. Jassy had been hankering after the main part but she was too ethereal, too small and dainty. She might have got away with it if her voice had carried better, which was the excuse Sally would have given – she would not have dreamed of saying she was just not a good enough actress to carry it off. Now it didn't matter, Jassy would never act again.

She went out to the garden which she and her husband had had landscaped. John had even built the small pond himself and had planted the weeping willow which was no longer a sapling and already trailed prettily. The sun beat down on the top of her head and made her feel sick and dizzy. No food had passed her lips for twenty-four hours, not since breakfast yesterday, and lack of sleep didn't help. She went back inside, grateful for the coolness of the lounge which the sun didn't reach until late afternoon. No sooner had she sat down than she heard a car door shutting. Although it had not been slammed the sound carried in the still air of the deserted road. Wearily she stood up, feeling far older than her twenty-seven years, and went to open the door to DC Brenda Gibbons.

'Mrs Foster? Sally Foster?' Brenda smiled encouragingly. If it had not been standard procedure to establish to whom she was talking, she would not have needed to ask. The woman's face showed exactly what she had been going through.

'Yes. Please come in.' Sally stepped back and opened the heavy wooden door to its full extent.

Brenda, identity in hand, introduced herself to the woman's retreating back as she followed her to the kitchen.

'I'll make us some tea.'

'Thank you.' It would give her something to do, distract her a little from what she had to say.

Brenda sat on one of the tubular steel chairs at the smoked glass table. As with Jassy and Joff's house, the whole of her own ground floor would fit into this kitchen. She crossed her tanned legs, flicked her long hair back over her shoulders and tucked her embroidered T-shirt more firmly into the waist of her skirt.

Two mugs, also smoked glass, were placed on the table along with a sugar bowl. 'No thanks, I've got these.' Brenda held up a container of sweeteners which she had taken from her large leather shoulder-bag. In front of her lay a notepad and pen. 'This isn't some sort of interrogation,' she began gently, seeing the startled expression on Mrs Foster's face when she saw the writing implements. 'In fact, it might be better if you just tell me what happened. Start from when you got up yesterday morning if it makes it any easier.'

Sally Foster nodded, but her mouth was working as she held back the tears. 'John went off to work. I tidied up a bit and did some washing. We've got someone who comes in once a week to hoover and dust, that sort of thing. Anyway, the weather was lovely so I sat outside for a while and read. I'd arranged to see Jassy, I'd . . .'

'It's all right, take your time.' Brenda looked away to give her time to compose herself.

'I'd planned to spend an hour or so with her, going over our next production. We belong to the Drama Guild. This year it was my turn to direct and cast the play. There were things I needed to discuss with her. She said we might as well have afternoon tea together as Joff was away, just strawberries, she said, and some dry white wine. It sounded nice, just the sort of thing Jassy would do, she was great at making small things seem like a treat. Afterwards I planned to think seriously about the casting.'

'It was your day off?' Brenda knew that, unlike Jasmine Grant, Mrs Foster had a full-time job. And she'd been at home, just around the corner in the next street. There was always the slimmest chance she'd seen something, something the shock she had received yesterday had prevented her from recalling. But Brenda was taking it gently. Sally Foster had explained how she had intended spending her day but she had left out the important part, how she actually did spend it.

'I was owed some time.'

'I see. What time did Jassy ask you to go round?'

Sally shrugged. Her large breasts wobbled beneath the thin material of her shirt. She was overweight but in a way Andrew Osborne would describe as pleasantly plump. Her face was round and open rather than pretty, but it was an unfair judgement to make because of the ravages of prolonged crying.

Ah, Andrew, Brenda thought, hoping she would finish in time to see him that evening.

'It was a fluid arrangement. Jassy was like that. She said to come whenever I wanted. As it didn't seem as if she'd got anything else planned, I thought about three o'clock.'

'So you walked up to Aspen Close and knocked on the door?' She would lead her slowly to the terrible scene which had awaited her.

'No. I went around the side, to the back door as I always do. It was open. Ajar. I pushed it and went in. I – oh, God, it was awful.'

Brenda didn't have a chance to say anything more because Sally lurched from the room, just making it to the downstiars cloakroom where she was sick. Brenda could hear her retching. When she came back her face was grey but she seemed more in control.

'Are you all right to go on?' Sally nodded and tried to smile. 'Think carefully, was there anything which struck you as unusual, either in the street or at Jassy's house?'

With a frown of concentration Sally shook her head. 'No, everything seemed the same as always. It's very quiet around here. I'm sure I'd've noticed anything different.'

'All right, what about Jassy herself?'

'I'm not sure. Maybe there was something. Oh, I'm probably imagining it because you asked, but she may have been a bit quieter recently. Mind you, I put that down to Joff going away. She said it would be the first time they'd spent a night apart since they'd been married, except when Joff was on nights but she didn't count that. She still saw him at both ends of the day.'

'Could they have argued about this trip?'

'Joff and Jassy? Never. He loves his fishing, she'd not have tried to stop him. She didn't want to go with him, though, she said she couldn't think of anything more boring.'

'When did you last see her – before yesterday, that is?'

'On Monday. We arrived home at the same time. We chatted in the road for a few minutes, that's all.'

'And how did she seem?'

Sally picked at a loose thread on the seam of her skirt. 'Now you mention it, she looked a bit, well, strained. It was unlike her, she was always so full of life.' Sally glanced up, her eyes wide. 'You don't think Joff was seeing someone else, do you? I mean, his going off like that wasn't an excuse?'

'No. We know he was where he said he was,' Brenda answered. 'I won't keep you any longer, Mrs Foster. Look, if anything else does occur to you, no matter how insignificant it may seem, please ring me. Here's my card.'

'Of course.' Sally got up and followed Brenda to the door. 'I'll go back to work tomorrow. I can't stay here, thinking about it.'

'It's probably for the best.' Brenda smiled and got back into the car, flinching at the heat, the steering wheel almost too hot to touch. What had been troubling Jassy Grant? Something they ought to know about, or was she simply tired or feeling the heat? Who was there who could answer that? Sally Foster had been her best friend but perhaps other friends at the tennis club or in the Drama Guild might know more. It wasn't always the people closest who were able to spot when things were not right.

Number three squad were working their way along Aspen Close following up the house-to-house inquiries. Many of the occupants were out at work during the day, and two families were away on holiday. According to neighbours both lots had been away for at least a week so could be ruled out as possible witnesses. By the end of Thursday squad number three knew no more than they had at the beginning – understandably, though, because the houses were large and detached and each was set back from the road and sheltered by high hedges and trees. No dogs had barked because only one resident owned one and, as luck would have it, it had been at the vet's for the previous two days. However, from the reactions they received, they were pretty certain that no one in Maple Drive had made that telephone call informing them of Petesy French's presence, using a false name. That, at least, meant something. Or did it?

Oliver Bilton-Jones and Richard Fry were lunching at the Taj Mahal as was par for the course on Thursdays. Fry, however, was eating a mushroom omelette and chips, much to the amusement of his companion who made fun of him on each visit. Fry found the smell of Indian food nauseating, the taste even worse, and he could not understand how anyone could bear to eat it in weather such as this. Wave upon wave of onion and garlic and spices wafted from the kitchen as the waiters pushed through the swing doors. There were always several full tables on a Thursday lunchtime, mostly occupied by businessmen.

'Are you sure he'll pay?'

Bilton-Jones looked up, a forkful of meat Madras half-way to his mouth. 'Of course he will. And you'll get your cut, just as I promised. Look, I really can't see why you're so bothered. The man has no choice, can't you see that? A large brandy, please.' He held up a hand to signal to the waiter then pushed his plate away, knife and fork neatly aligned down the centre. All that was left were a few grains of rice and some orangey-red greasy smears.

'And for you, sir?' The waiter inclined his head towards Fry.

'Not for me thanks.' Fry was driving.

Bilton-Jones nodded towards Fry's plate where the congealed egg and greasy chips lay half eaten. 'Not hungry?'

'Too hot.'

Bilton-Jones smiled. It was mirthless. It wasn't the food, he knew that, Fry lived on a diet of greasy junk food. Nevertheless, 'too hot' was probably an appropriate phrase for how he was feeling. It was something he would have to get used to if he wanted the money. And he did want it. He knew how much Fry wanted to get married to that sexy little Stephanie Deakon, although heaven knows why anyone should wish a noose around his neck. To be fair, Steph wasn't at all bad-looking and she seemed equally fond of Richard. But to Oliver Bilton-Jones any female who did not come from a class family wasn't worth knowing. His own wife, Hilary, had been to the right schools and knew how to entertain and how to dress. Never had he had to suffer the embarrassment of sitting in a restaurant and waiting for her to pick up the wrong piece of cutlery. These things mattered to him and Hilary would not let him down even if she had put on a bit of weight and refused to do anything with her unruly mousy hair which billowed around her face and shoulders just as it had done when she was a student. Bilton-Jones had no idea that Richard Fry was simply waiting until he had enough saved to put down a deposit on a small house. When the time came he intended moving as far away from Rickenham Green as possible, taking Steph with him. Then he would go straight. With this latest job, once they had been paid for it, he would have reached his target and he'd never have to kowtow to the likes of Bilton-Jones again. He accepted that for the moment they must carry on as usual, but it was only for another week. He felt sick with excitement.

Bilton-Jones was ready to leave. He drained his brandy glass as he got to his feet. Richard followed him out of the restaurant where the heat shimmered over the tarmac and enveloped him. He could smell curry on his clothes and something awful from a drain. The omelette lay heavily in his stomach.

'Where now?' he asked once Bilton-Jones had strapped himself into the passenger seat.

'Where else? Usual Thursday afternoon run, Richard.'

Markham spent the morning at the tennis club, which was not at all his scene and precisely why DCI Roper had delegated those particular interviews to him. Shouts could be heard from the courts and most of the members were dressed in the obligatory white, ranging from knee-length shorts to tiny pleated skirts. Some people were seated at wrought iron tables, soft drinks in front of them, as they waited for a court to become free. The women outnumbered the men but there were enough of the latter for Markham to wonder what kind of jobs they had to enable them to sit around on a Thursday afternoon. He had spoken to a man in a blazer with a gold embroidered badge on the pocket before he had been allowed in, quietly explaining his reason for being there. The man had obligingly said he would ask the members to come to him one by one so he could ask his questions. He was then shown into a small room, presumably used for card games as the walls were lined with tables covered in green baize. Unlike the Elms, there was no waiting list here – in fact the newly formed club was advertising for members. There were fewer than seventy registered, Markham had learned.

Gazing out of the window at the twenty or so people idling at the tables or smashing a ball across the net, Markham was aware that one or two glances were being directed his way. Good. They were curious. However, they could not be unaware of the reason for his visit. The local news had carried the story and it had merited a few words on the national news, no doubt because Jasmine Grant was the wife of a policeman. The blazored Jeremy Ferguson moved briskly over the concrete paving stones which formed the terrace.

Despite the heat and his bulk he moved with grace, one of those short, plump men who would glide across a dance floor. His smiles were conciliatory as he spoke briefly to each party. Markham saw Ferguson nod in his direction to a tall skinny female who stood up and made her way towards the clubhouse. A few seconds later there was a knock at the door.

'Come in.'

'Jeremy said you wanted to speak to me.'

Markham turned around slowly. The woman reddened and automatically checked the hemline of her short skirt as he looked her up and down, although there was nothing lascivious in his appraisal – he was merely mentally recording her description. 'You are?'

'Philippa Jackson but most people call me Pippa.'

Markham indicated one of the hard-backed chairs he had pulled out from beneath a table. Pippa Jackson hesitated before taking it. She crossed then uncrossed her long legs, aware of the shortness of her skirt.

'Why you? First, I mean?'

'Because Jeremy knows I was closer to Jassy than the others. She was a new member here but I've known her for a long time.'

This was not news. The woman's number had been in Jassy's diary listed under the name Pippa. The lack of a surname suggested they were friends.

'How long?'

'Since school.'

Markham thought she seemed nervous but his presence often produced that effect. Her neck was beginning to show signs of crepiness and the blackness of her hair was unnatural and unflattering. If she was a contemporary of the dead woman she had not worn at all well. Nervousness aside, he wondered why, if they had been friends, Philippa Jackson did not appear unduly upset.

'Since school. That's a long time.' He allowed a second or two for his meaning to sink in.

'I know it must seem awful, me being here so soon after

it's happened, but I couldn't see the point in staying at home brooding.'

'But Mrs Grant was your friend.'

She flushed again, her skin mottling pinkly. 'I didn't say that exactly.'

'Then what, exactly, are you saying?'

'We were at school together, but not in the same class. I'm two years older than Jassy. Our parents were friends, we were sort of thrown together.'

'And after you left school?'

'Jassy went abroad for a while, she didn't enjoy it much. I'd have loved to have gone. Still, water under the bridge. We kept in touch. Neither of us moved away like most of the people we knew. It was habit more than anything else.'

'But you met socially?'

'Yes. Sometimes.'

'Mrs Jackson, what can you tell me about Mrs Grant? Was she popular as a member here?'

'You mean, do I know who might have wanted to kill her? Then the answer's no.'

'But it doesn't answer my question.'

Pippa Jackson crossed her legs again, this time less self-consciously, and studied her fingernails. 'Everybody liked her. She was always smiling. Even the women weren't resentful.'

'Why should they be?' Markham knew, but he wanted to hear her say it. Pippa Jackson, he guessed, had been jealous of her friend.

'Because she was beautiful and because their husbands always made a point of speaking to her.'

'Anyone more than the others?'

The laugh was brittle but it told Markham what he needed to know. 'Good God, no. This is Jassy we're talking about. She could do no wrong.'

'Except in your eyes?'

'What?'

'Why didn't you like her?'

'I did. I tried so hard. It wasn't like you think. You see, I knew she used me. She was always the pretty one, the one with the latest clothes and the best-looking men. I was her foil. I knew it. I've always known it but there was something about her that was irresistible. If she wanted to see me I always agreed. I did like her,' Pippa added quietly, 'but I always wished she had liked me more.'

Markham believed her. The plain, old-before-her-time Mrs Jackson had been used to highlight Jassy's good points. It was not information which would necessarily lead to her murderer but it shed a new light on the almost-perfect Jasmine Grant. 'What else did she do, apart from play tennis?'

'She was involved in a drama group – that took up quite a lot of her time. Once a week she went to see her parents and she was forever making alterations at home. You know, new wallpaper or curtains, that sort of thing. She was never bored. I don't work, sergeant, but there're times when I wish I did. My husband takes pride in the fact that I don't need to. It's ridiculous in this day and age, but then, he's quite a few years older than me.' Markham was about to interrupt but the woman was less tense, he might learn something. 'I think that's another reason why Jassy continued seeing me. There aren't many women of our age who stay at home, not unless they've got children, and they're too busy to do the things we enjoyed. Don't get me wrong, Jassy's case was different. She had no intention of getting a job. She told me that more than once. She said she wanted to get the most out of her youth.' Pippa frowned. 'She also said she had no intention of ruining her figure by having children, at least, not in the foreseeable future.'

So Jassy Grant was vain. It fell into place. The unattractive girlfriends, the Drama Guild where her charms could be displayed to their full on stage, the lack of contact with Flora, her sister, who was equally beautiful and who held down a well-paid and demanding job and who might steal her thunder. Markham was beginning to get the feeling that Jassy

Grant had remained a spoiled and pampered child. Hardly a motive for someone to kill her, though.

'I couldn't understand it. I'd give anything to be able to have a baby.'

Markham turned away, uncomfortable with the intimate words yet feeling unusual sympathy for the woman he was interviewing. 'I'm sorry,' he murmured.

'It's not even as if it's my husband's fault, if that's the word. Forgive me. I'm not here to tell you all this.'

It seemed to have done her good. Her skin was now a normal tone, slightly tanned, and the bitterness had left her voice.

'Mrs Grant was a fairly new member here – do you think anyone else knew her well?'

'It's difficult to say. I don't know everyone myself yet, the place has only been going a few months. A lot of the members are middle-aged, and some have joined to meet people because they're new to the area. I doubt if anyone knew her as well as me.

'I introduced Jassy. She asked me to. I don't think she was close to anyone else here but I can't be certain.'

'Mrs Grant was a local girl. Why do you think she didn't apply for membership as soon as she knew the club was opening?'

'I've no idea. Oh, I see. You think she wanted to wait for everyone else to join then make an entrance on her own?'

'Do you?'

A small sigh was followed with the sadly spoken words, 'I think it's highly likely.'

Markham managed one of his less intimidating smiles. 'Mrs Jackson, you've been extremely helpful. You can go now. Thank you.'

She stood up awkwardly, almost knocking her chair over but catching it in time. 'Would you like me to send anyone else in?'

'No, that won't be necessary.' He had a good idea that all

he would hear from the male contingent would be eulogies while the females would want to prove how welcome they had tried to make Jassy feel even if they'd hated her guts. Besides, Jeremy Ferguson, in his badge and blazer, symbols of clubmen and committee men everywhere, might appear a little pompous, officious even, but Markham would bet that he knew his members and what went on amongst them. Why else send Philippa Jackson in first? He would have a few words with Ferguson and leave it at that. Discreet inquiries had shown it was highly unlikely that either Joff or Jassy was involved with anyone else; with Joff particularly, it would have been almost impossible for someone not to have known, the station being the source of gossip that it was.

Markham strolled out on to the terrace, mindless of the sun beating down on his head. Ferguson was leaning on the back of a seat, chatting to its occupant.

'Could I have a word?'

'Of course. Of course.' He followed Markham back into the card room.

'Mrs Jackson has been very helpful.' Markham hoped he would relay this back to the woman – it might cheer her up a little.

'Good. Good. I would hate to think that one of our members was in any way obstructing the police in their duties.'

One of those, Markham thought. A man who made it his business to show what a good citizen he was. So be it. He would probably tell the truth. 'How well did you know Mrs Grant?'

'Apart from Pippa, as well as anyone else. Jassy was one of our newest members. She mixed well, a social animal I'd say. She was liked by almost everybody.'

'But not by you?'

'Oh dear, oh dear.' Ferguson coughed to cover his embarrassment. He had not lied but he had not expected that his qualification would be jumped on so readily.

'Well?'

'Don't misunderstand, I don't mean I actively disliked her.'

74

'But?'

Ferguson shrugged; he was finding it hard going. 'I don't know, and that's the truth. I just felt there was something . . . well, something not quite genuine about her. I'm probably wrong. Yes, probably wrong. Just an old fool.'

'I doubt that, sir. Perhaps you could tell me what it was that made you feel that way?'

Ferguson indicated the vacant seat. 'May I?' Markham nodded but retained his own position, arms folded, legs crossed at the ankles, his buttocks resting on the white-painted windowsill. 'I'm not sure that anyone can explain such feelings. Jassy was undoubtedly beautiful, unfailingly pleasant and cheerful, and that's good for the club, of course. No moods or sulkiness. As a tennis player she was quite good and I think she could've been better but she wasn't interested in lessons with the pro.'

'Why not?'

'Well, I got the impression . . . God, this is so difficult. Some of the women, you see, well, and Jassy . . .'

'You think she believed she might attract gossip if she took lessons?'

'Yes. Quite. Quite. Our Dave is just the sort of man who appeals to some of the, shall we say, older women?'

Markham got the picture, or thought he had until Ferguson continued speaking.

'It wasn't so much that she was afraid of what people might say about her – she made it known that she was devoted to her husband. It was more . . . well, to be honest, I felt it was an act.'

'Mr Ferguson, please be more explicit.'

'All right. I'll put my cards on the table.' He seemed not to notice the appropriateness of his words considering where they were. 'By subtle means she let it be known that she had no intention of making the women less blessed in the looks department jealous by flirting with their husbands or spending time with Dave. Does that answer your question?'

'Yes. Anything else?'

'No. As I said, these are merely my feelings and I've probably misread her completely. As to knowing her on a personal level, I didn't. I only ever saw her here. I'd heard of the family, naturally – having one of them as a member was good for the club. And as to why anyone wanted to murder her, I've no idea. No idea at all.'

'Thanks for your co-operation, Mr Ferguson.' Those who knew Markham would have been amazed at his tact.

'Don't you want to speak to anyone else?'

'No, I don't think that'll be necessary.'

Ferguson held out a hand then quickly withdrew it, unsure of the form with a member of the police. 'I'll . . . ah, I'll be on my way then.'

Markham watched him go. Jasmine Grant was vain and she was manipulative. How much more was there to learn, how many reasons might there be for wishing her dead? Other heads were needed here, ones who had spoken to the rest of Jassy's friends and acquaintances. Together they might build up a complete picture. All Markham had gleaned was envy on the part of Pippa Jackson and the possible imaginings of Jeremy Ferguson. Yet he would bet Ferguson was a good judge of character.

5

DS Barry Swan couldn't face lunch. Having gone over his caseload he returned to the flat and double-checked that everything was ready. The cot was assembled although Lucy had said that the baby would initially sleep in the carry cot in their bedroom. They had planned to move after the birth of the child they lost and had not wanted to tempt fate by doing so before this one was safely born, but they must start making serious plans as soon as his transfer had come through.

This one. Unnamed as yet. He hoped Lucy would come up with something suitable for their son.

'Our son.' The words still sounded strange.

Barry walked around the spacious lounge and thought how pleased Lucy would be with his attempt at dusting and the flowers he had stuck in a vase on the high mantelpiece. Her parents had been to the hospital but had returned to Bury St Edmunds until their daughter was discharged. There was no room for them in the flat so they had booked a week at the Duke of Clarence, the best hotel in Rickenham Green, which, he thought uncharitably, they could afford, and would be coming over each day to help out once she was home. One thing was certain, they would not be allowed to spoil the boy. Only now did the sadness of his own state register – he had no family to share his joy. His father had served in the diplomatic corps and his mother had travelled with him. Barry had been brought up by his maternal grandmother whose flat he had inherited. Now both his parents were dead, killed dramatically by a terrorist's bomb. They had not met Lucy because they had not lived to make it back for their wedding. But tonight he would have his self-made family and, for the moment, that was all that mattered.

At three thirty he drove across the town and out on to the ring road to Rickenham General. The car-seat was fixed into place, the hospital had insisted this was so before the baby could leave. It was on the front seat, facing away from the windscreen, but could be removed whenever necessary.

Through the door of the modern unit with its pastel colours and duvet-covered beds he saw Lucy, dressed and ready, her case at her feet, the baby in her arms. She was smiling. A nurse came with them to the car.

Once they were settled he started the engine, grimacing at the noise and checking to see that he had not woken his son.

'He has to get used to it. I want him to be able to sleep through anything. Especially the night,' she added, having had some experience of two o'clock feeds.

She was grinning as he helped her out of the back seat before unstrapping the baby.

'What is it?'

'You. I don't think you exceeded fifteen miles an hour all the way back.'

Barry fiddled with the baby's straps and hoped he'd become more adept quickly. There was a handle to the car-seat which meant he could carry the baby upstairs in it.

'Oh, it's good to be home. It feels as if I've been gone for a month. Just stick him on the floor,' she said casually.

Barry did so, very gently, beside the settee and out of the way of their feet. He was nonplussed at Lucy's sureness when dealing with the child. 'Tea?'

'Love some. Then you can tell me what I've been missing.'

She knew, of course, about Jasmine Grant. Like Moira Roper she had met her socially on a few occasions but her own life was too full to grieve much.

'There's not much to tell, really. For obvious reasons,' Barry nodded towards the car-seat where the child still slept, 'I'm not on the team. Joff's staying with the Bakers.'

'What about his family?'

'They're not local. Apparantly he doesn't want them here.'

Lucy found this strange but did not comment. She sipped the tea and lay back against the cushions of her chair. Her face was pale, her tan had already begun to fade and she was more tired than she cared to admit. 'Oh, hell.'

'What is it?' Barry was on his feet at once. 'Is something wrong? Do you hurt?'

'No. I was just looking at my stomach. I hope it doesn't take too long to flatten. Anyway, did I mention Moira's coming over later?'

'No.' Barry was disappointed but Moira had been more than a friend, especially when things had gone wrong the last time.

'She promised she wouldn't stay long. And she's bringing a bottle of wine.'

'Should you . . .?'

'Yes. I've been abstemious quite long enough.'

It took Lucy, with Barry's help, the next hour and a half to feed and change the baby. What had seemed so simple in the unit, with everything to hand, was a major operation. 'Right, tomorrow you can get me a pretty plastic bag, a hold-all or something. I'm going to keep everything all in one place. Look, he's going to sleep again.' The doorbell rang and they both held their breath but the tiny eyelids only fluttered before closing again.

'He's gorgeous,' Moira whispered, bending over the pram in which the baby had been placed. Already he seemed to have taken over the room.

'No need to whisper. He's got to get used to noise.'

'No name yet?'

'No. Barry, go and open whatever it is Moira's clutching so tightly.'

'My pleasure.'

Lucy pushed back her brown hair. It was a bit lank but later she would have a bath and wash it. Everything seemed such an effort at the moment. 'I bet you're glad you don't have all this to go through again. Oh, Moira – I didn't mean that how it sounded.'

'I know. But you're right, I couldn't bear the thought now of all those years of motherhood again. I wish we'd had a second one, though.'

'Well, you can babysit any time.'

'Here, you shouldn't have been so extravagant.' Barry returned bearing a tray and three glasses containing champagne.

They chatted, at first about the baby and then, as almost always happened, about work. 'I've missed it in a way, not being in on things. Still, young whatshisname more than makes up for it.'

'Well, here's to whatshisname.' Moira raised her glass.

'Did I tell you what happened to me the other night? It's

his fault, mind you.' Barry gestured towards the baby. 'I walked out of the Taj Mahal without paying. No one stopped me, I was half-way home before I remembered.'

'You've told me that twice already,' Lucy said. 'It's no big deal, you went back and paid.'

Moira smiled. Despite Barry Swan's public persona she knew this would have embarrassed him deeply. 'Well, don't tell Ian. Free curries would be his idea of paradise.'

Barry had told Ian, who had not been listening.

'I'm going now. You two can finish the champagne.'

'There's no need.'

'No, but you look tired, Lucy, and you need some time together. Just give me a ring if you want anything, shopping or a bit of company.' She stood and smoothed down the skirt of her cotton dress which had creased during the course of the day. 'Are you back at work tomorrow?' she asked Barry.

'Yes. I'm taking my leave in odd days.'

Moira bent over the pram and planted a light kiss on the downy head sleeping there. 'Bye-bye, whatshisname.'

'Martin,' Barry said unexpectedly.

'Pardon?' Moira straightened up again.

'Martin, after my father.'

'Yes,' Lucy said. 'That's perfect.' She knew what it would mean to Barry and she liked the name. 'Martin *Ian* Swan.'

'What?' Moira and Barry spoke together.

'Ian, after your bad-tempered husband.'

'The poor wee thing.' But she was pleased on his behalf. Ian might only grunt when he heard but would be delighted all the same.

She drove home thoughtfully, wondering if she would see her husband at all that evening.

Ian sent down to the canteen for a sandwich and some black coffee. The heat had dulled his appetite but his waistband was looser which was no bad thing. It was far too early for lunch but he had eaten so little over the past forty-eight hours that his capability for clear thinking would be impaired if he didn't get some sustenance. It had been agreed that Ian should see Joff personally and informally, and as a matter of courtesy. He had checked with Bill Baker and knew that Avril would be out of the house until at least four fifteen; although Bill was off duty that afternoon he had said there were things he needed to do in Rickenham Green before returning home.

Ian chewed his sandwich, hardly tasting it, then threw most of the second half into the bin. Impatient for news he strode down to the incident room only to learn that Markham was not yet back from the tennis club, number three squad was still in Maple Grove and DC Gibbons had not returned from Sally Foster's. To the astonishment of many, Petesy French had been released. Just like that. They had not charged him and the time they were allowed to hold him without doing so had expired. It was the Chief Constable's decision to let him go. Having talked it over with Superintendent Thorne they had agreed that he might be more use out on the streets than locked up in a cell. Opinion was still equally divided as to whether French was capable of such a crime, and French was unaware that he had been put under twenty-four-hour surveillance.

'You see, Ian,' Mike Thorne had said to Ian earlier, 'if we take it that the gun was planted, then we have to assume that very shortly after the crime took place French was in the company of whoever placed it in his hold-all. And if you take into account the anonymous telephone call then, as you quite rightly pointed out, someone wanted French to be found near the scene and in possession of the firearm, which implies that he was meant to carry the can. And that someone probably knows he's got a record of sorts. If we're right, someone's going to get a nasty shock when they see French back on the streets. If we're wrong we can pick him up again. At least it's not our necks on the line, this is down to the CC.'

And, thinking about it, Ian had to agree it was a good idea. There was, however, one flaw. If French *was* guilty they were going to look idiots in the eyes of the general public.

As he reluctantly got back into his car to make his way to the Bakers' house, DCI Roper received a radio message to say that Brenda Gibbons had left Sally Foster's and wanted to know if she should make a start on the Drama Guild. Ian told her to go ahead. By the end of the day the people closest to Jasmine Grant would all have been interviewed.

It was a strange sensation for Ian as he pulled up in the street of terraced housing. He was about to enter the home of a fellow policeman, one he knew relatively well, but whose house he had never set foot in before. But Bill and Avril Baker were not at home, it was another policeman he was calling to see, one whose wife had recently been murdered.

He had to ring the bell twice. When Joff came to the door it was obvious that he had been sitting outside. He was bare-chested and his skin had that warm sunshine smell. His body was fit and tanned but his face told a different story. There were purple smudges beneath his red-rimmed eyes and the pupils were dull as if the life had gone out of them. Joff Grant looked a beaten man.

'Come on in, sir.'

'Thank you.' Ian followed him out to the kitchen where an empty mug stood on the table. It was otherwise immaculate.

'I was sitting outside, trying to think. It's impossible. All I can see is her face.'

'You know why I'm here.'

'Yes, sir.'

Ian had decided to avoid sympathy. Joff's colleagues had been unanimous when they said he would want to be treated as any other husband of a murdered wife. He was that sort of a man. They were stunned, unable to imagine what this would do to him, he and Jassy had been so close.

'Have you had a chance to make out a list?'

'Yes.' Joff reached into his hip pocket and pulled out a crumpled piece of paper. There were many names written on it. 'Family first, relationship next to the names, then close friends, acquaintances, and lastly tennis club and Drama Guild. I don't know the names of everyone she knew at the last two.' It was a comprehensive list. He paused. 'It gave me something to do, took my mind off things for half an hour.'

'Of course. Thank you.'

'Can I get you some tea, sir?'

'No, I'm fine, thanks.' It was a weird situation. Someone should have been offering PC Grant tea but it seemed inappropriate for Ian to do so in somebody else's kitchen. 'Can we go over your movements during the last week? There might be something . . .'

'You don't have to explain. I know I'm the first in line.'

Had Joff forgotten Petesy French? He could not know he had been released.

'I left to go on the trip. God, how I wish I hadn't. Jassy wasn't all that happy about it, not that she asked me not to go, nothing like that, but I knew. It was the first time we'd been apart, you see. Anyway, I was met at Edinburgh, it was part of the deal, and, along with some of the others, driven to the hotel where we were staying. The first night we just sat around getting to know each other. We had a meal and a few drinks but everyone was too tired to stay up late. Most of us had had a long journey.

'The next morning the minibus took us to – '

'Joff, forget the trip. Tell me about before you went.' Both men were still standing. Ian drew out a chair and waved a hand for Joff to do the same.

'There's nothing to tell. Jassy played tennis and visited her parents and saw her friends. The usual things. I was on earlies. We spent the evenings together.'

'And you were expecting Jassy to meet you?'

Joff frowned, wondering how they knew. 'Yes. I wrote down the train times for her. As it was such a long journey I told her to ring first to make sure the train was running on time before she set out.'

'You changed trains?'

'Only the once. It was easier to go straight into London, then get a tube to Liverpool Street for the Ipswich train.'

And the train had been on time, Brenda could bear that out.

'What about the night before you left?' He had almost said 'your last night together'.

Joff looked exhausted. 'We didn't do anything special. We sat in the garden and read then had something to eat and watched a bit of television. You know, all those normal things that make up a happy marriage, things you take for granted until they're snatched away from you.' Joff's face was red as he brushed tears from his eyes angrily.

Ian nodded. He did know and he tried not to take them for granted where Moira was concerned, but he often failed.

Joff shook his head as if to clear it of those last images. 'We went to bed about ten because I'd got an early start. That's it.'

'The return journey – did the minibus take you back to Waverley station?'

'No. We were all setting off at different times, we had to make our own arrangements.'

Ian chewed the inside of his mouth. He hated having to ask but it was necessary that he did so. 'What were your arrangements?'

'I booked a taxi. It seemed the easiest thing to do.' His head dropped forward and he squeezed his eyelids between thumb and forefinger, stemming more tears. 'Bill Baker and his wife have been great. I couldn't have gone back to the house and there was nowhere else to go.'

'Don't you think it might be a good idea to get away from here for a while? How about your parents?'

'No.'

Ian waited but there was no further explanation. 'Any other relatives?'

'Not close ones, and I don't want them here, sir.'

There was nothing Ian could say to that. Blood was not, as many people believed, thicker than water. 'Fair enough. Have you spoken to Jassy's parents yet?'

'Yes. I rang this morning. It was awful, one of the hardest

things I've ever had to do. None of us knew what to say to each other.'

'Just a couple more questions, Joff. Oh, listen to me. You know the form well enough. Did Jassy seem worried about anything recently?'

'No. Once or twice she was a bit quiet, but that was because I was going away. I should never have left her alone.'

'I checked your rota, Joff – you'd have been on duty if you weren't away.' It was small consolation for a man in his position.

'Why her? What harm's Jassy ever done anyone?'

We don't know yet, Ian thought, but random killings are few and far between. And unless she had been living a double life the chances of her knowing Petesy French were minimal.

'I can't stay here for ever,' Joff continued. 'I suppose I'll have to go back to the house at some point. Is it . . . I mean . . . Oh, shit.' He ran a hand angrily through his hair.

'Tomorrow, Joff. You can go home tomorrow.' Forensics might need more time although Ian suspected they had done everything possible. What he wanted to ensure was that no signs of the brutal killing remained, no fingerprint dust or bloodstains to make it harder for Joff. The kitchen, however, might still be out of bounds.

'That's it, Joff. If there's anything we can do, you know where to find us.'

'Thank you, sir.'

He didn't get up as Ian made his way to the front door of the small house. Looking back once, he saw the younger man slumped over the table, his head in his hands.

Joff was nowhere near coming to terms with his loss and Ian had not expected it to be a fruitful interview but the motions had to be gone through. He wound down the car windows and headed back to the station. Between the buildings he noticed the strange colour of the sky. No breeze stirred, there was nothing to alleviate the heavy, headache-producing humidity.

Along the pavements pedestrians moved slowly, as if

walking through the oppressive heat was an effort. An elderly man, wearing a linen cap, stopped to wipe his brow with a checked handkerchief. A woman pushing a pram slowly overtook the man. An older child stood on the footrest, facing his mother, and a third child was attached to her wrist by way of a strap. Rolls of flesh were visible through the tight-fitting stretchy dress and her arms wobbled with the movement of the pram. She still looked pregnant; the baby must be very young. Lucy would not let herself go like that, any more than Moira had. Ian stifled the unfair thought. The woman had three children and he knew nothing of her circumstances. Was it a blessing that the Grants had had no children, or would Joff have preferred a permanent reminder of his wife?

Over forty-eight hours had passed. The crucial hours. The more time that elapsed, the less chance they had of finding the killer.

The school holidays were dragging to an end so there was not the usual volume of mid-afternoon term-time traffic. In fact, Ian thought, the streets seemed almost as quiet as they had done in the days when Rickenham had a half-day and the shops shut for lunch. It was the weather keeping people at home or taking them to the coast, away from the fumes and claustrophia of the buildings. Children would be jumping in and out of paddling pools if they were lucky, or the sea if they were luckier still. Those who lived in places like Magnolia House on the high rise estate would have to make do with the dust bowl of the communal lawn.

'Why is the world such a godawful place?' Ian muttered as he indicated to turn into the station car-park. Above, the sky was sulphurous and heat shimmered in the air, blurring the outlines of the baking metal of the cars. The tarmac was sticky beneath his feet and his body was wet with sweat. For once the air-conditioning would be welcome and he would not abuse the notices requesting that windows be kept shut.

Both DS Markham and DC Gibbons had returned and

were comparing notes in the incident room. 'Anything new?' Ian asked optimistically.

'No, sir, not unless you count a slightly different angle on the victim as important.'

'Oh?'

Markham seemed content to let Brenda do the talking. 'It seems, from what people have told us, that Jassy never really grew up. She comes across as one of those people who seek attention – well, need it, to be more accurate.'

'Well, she's getting it now.' Ian's bitterness was due to disappointment. 'Anyway, where's Campbell? I thought he was supposed to be part of this team.'

'He's visiting the male members of the Drama Guild. I thought if there was anything amiss they'd be more likely to confide in another male. I've got a message for him about the ABHs.'

'Hanson's dealing with them, not Campbell.'

'I know, sir, but Alan asked for any information to be passed on.'

'Campbell did?' It was enough to distract Ian from the seriousness of the business in hand. It was so unlike DC Alan Campbell – meticulous though he was, he was not renowned for being able to do two things at once or, as in this case, to think for himself.

'Another man's been attacked.'

'When?'

'Last night, sir. A man by the name of Sidiqi; somewhere between ten fifteen and ten thirty when he left his premises. It's a video and off-licence place. He had the takings on him but nothing was stolen and there's nothing to suggest it was a racial attack either.'

'Do we know that for certain?' It hadn't happened yet. There were two Chinese families who were rarely seen outside their restaurants apart from regular forays to the betting shop but they had been accepted into the town long ago. More recently had come the Asians, who tended to work long hours running their various businesses. It was the lack of motorways in Suffolk which had stemmed the tide of progress – the consequent lack of industrial jobs discouraged people from moving to the area. It would happen eventually, of course, but Ian hoped he did not live long enough to see the day when Rickenham Green became just like every other town and city. Naturally they did not live in isolation; more and more youths were drinking and the drug problem was growing and the blame had been heaped upon everybody but those responsible, the parents and the culprits themselves. The teenagers complained that there was nothing to do, that they were bored. The same complaint came from city kids where there were more amenities. There was a sports complex now and the coast was not many miles away where, for the price of a bus fare, they could spend a whole day. But no, they preferred to skateboard down the High Street and hang around aimlessly at nights. They've got it all wrong, Ian decided. They've got too much with their pocket money and computer games rather than too little. 'Oh, God.'

'Sir?' Brenda, head on one side, was half smiling at his expression.

'This bloody modern world.'

'There've always been murders.' She knew his moods so did not add that his was not the first generation to make such a complaint.

'Yes. Of course.' Ian straightened up. He was not about to tell these younger officers what really bothered him. On more than one occasion Moira had told him he was beginning to sound like his father. It was not a flattering observation. 'So what we have is this.' He ticked the points off on his fingers. 'Nothing from number three squad, nothing from the tennis club and nothing from the Drama Guild or the neighbour, Sally Foster.' Brenda nodded ruefully. 'No one's seen or heard anything, no one knows a thing. Brilliant.'

'But we know a little more about the girl's character.' This from Markham who dealt in facts.

The girl, Ian noticed. Already Joff Grant's wife had become

88

a statistic. Perhaps it was better that way, perhaps their involvement had been preventing them from seeing things objectively. Ian had realised that danger from the start. 'All right, Markham, get yourself back down to the Black Horse and rattle the landlord's cage a little. I don't suppose that'll be a hardship.' Markham took himself off immediately, glad to be out of the building once more. 'Brenda, you go and see the Goodwins. They should be up to answering some questions by now. Who's free to go with you?'

'Alan Campbell should be here soon. Shall I wait for him?'

'Yes, that's fine. As long as it's no more than ten minutes. I'll be here for the next couple of hours. I want to see what the obs team come up with.' Moira, he thought, I must ring her. Was it tonight she was going to see Lucy and the baby? He couldn't remember. He'd leave a message anyway. Brenda too, he noticed, had reached for a telephone but turned her back after she had dialled a number. Andrew Osborne? he wondered. If so, it must be serious. A strange choice, too. Brenda, so lithe and lovely with hair and teeth and a complexion that radiated good health, and a worn-down solicitor who, to Ian's mind, was positively ugly and whose face bore the scars of acne or chicken pox. However, it was not his concern.

That same shiny hair swung across her shoulders as she turned to greet DC Campbell.

As pale as ever, his skin gingerly freckled, he strolled into the general office shaking his head. 'I can't get anything out of any of them. They've nothing but good to say about Jassy. They didn't know that Sally Foster had arranged to see her to discuss the casting, not that it seems relevant.'

Ian sighed heavily. It was more or less what he had been expecting. 'Go with Brenda to the Goodwins'. Try and find out something we don't know. Any bloody thing at all. The sister's there. Flora. They seem to have a thing about flowers. Anyway, see what you can do.'

DC Campbell had spent the morning running checks on callers in the vicinity of Aspen Close – postmen, meter-reading men, milkmen – but he had drawn a blank. This was an area where his pedantry and doggedness paid off. If Alan Campbell said none of them had visited the house, then none had.

The names in the diary used as an address book matched those of her friends at the various clubs to which she belonged, and if something untoward had been going on in Jasmine Grant's life then it was hardly likely that she would have kept a record of it.

Brenda slung her bag over her shoulder and headed for the door. Alan started to follow her.

'Oh, the ABHs. There's a message for you. What's your interest?'

Alan Campbell's face turned scarlet. 'I'm not sure yet, sir. I'd already received the message, though. DC Hanson's dealing with the Sidiqi attack.'

Ian watched them leave. Campbell was not at all himself. It must be the heat.

6

'Wait.' Oliver Bilton-Jones laid a hand on Richard Fry's arm as they were about to step out of the car, legally parked in an indentation outside the Black Horse in Saxborough Road. 'There's French. Petesy French.'

'What's he doing out?'

'I doubt very much he slipped between the bars when they weren't looking. He hasn't been charged. Not yet. My guess is they're tailing him.'

Fry put the key back into the ignition and started the engine.

'What're you doing?'

'Getting out of here.'

'Did I ask you to? Don't be ridiculous. We've already discussed this, we carry on as normal.'

Fry sighed. He was hot and tired and he fancied a drink but he wouldn't be able to have one until he'd delivered Oliver home. Oliver looked far less in need of refreshment. His clothes were uncrumpled and his aftershave still gave off a pleasant faint scent. But as for discussing things, that was ridiculous. Bilton-Jones made the decisions and told him what they were.

Together they crossed the road, stopping on the small island in the middle to allow the traffic to pass. Dust flew into their faces, blown up by the slipstream of the fast-moving cars.

The door and windows of the Black Horse were open but the fuggy humidity remained, thick with the smell of fried food. With no air currents to disturb them wreaths of smoke drifted to the ceiling.

Petesy French was at the bar. In front of him was a pint of lager and a large Scotch, his massive hangover now a thing of the past, although he still did not understand how he had got into that state.

'So they let you go, then?' Oliver asked with a smile barely more than a sneer.

'Of course they did. I didn't do it. I soon showed them they couldn't hold me.' Petesy drew himself up to his full five feet six inches. Behind him Tony Peak raised his eyes then closed them. The man would live on this for ages, swaggering and boasting about how he outwitted the law. And, as they had agreed at lunchtime, Petesy might be stupid, he might also commit petty crimes, but no one could really picture him as a murderer.

Richard Fry reached for his tomato juice with Worcester sauce and added a handful of ice to make it last longer. He was glad Petesy hadn't been arrested. It didn't make sense, not about the gun. Not that he dared ask. In fact he had not asked about anything and he was beginning to wonder just how deeply he was involved. All he wanted now was the money in his hand and he'd be off; money he had been promised for acquiring the gun from an associate of his in Birmingham. Oliver could then drive his own sodding car and get someone else to run his errands. He had been used but he was fair-minded enough to recognise that, in turn, he had used Oliver.

'Ah, one of our respected officers of the law.' Bilton-Jones nudged Fry. Markham had just walked in. No one was unduly worried, Markham had used the pub for as long as the rest of them and he didn't bring his work into the social arena. Or so they thought.

Markham approached the bar, not at all surprised to see French there ahead of him. He nodded to the people he knew then ordered his drink and paid for it.

'Same again, please, Tony,' Bilton-Jones said pleasantly as he slid a note across the bar.

Tony Peak refilled their glasses. Something was going on here – he sensed it but did not understand what it was. He handed over the change and went to serve another customer.

When Oliver had finished his drink he gave Fry the signal that he was ready to leave. Thursday night, the same as usual, two drinks then off. And Tony Peak guessed where they would be going. Bilton-Jones had let it be known that he made his money from his fleet of container lorries which transported frozen foods, and so he did, but not all of it. However, with the hours Tony kept he was hardly in a position to throw stones.

Outside, in the car, Oliver handed Fry a fifty-pound note on account but nothing was said by either man.

Markham saw them leave but kept his eyes to the front. Petesy French was ignoring him, which was good; he did not want to get into a discussion about his arrest, and the observation team would do their thing. Mark Howard came in, grinning when he saw Petesy. Markham knew his reputation as a fence, a man as incompetent as French with whom he was now in a huddle, no doubt going over Petesy's experiences in the nick. A couple sat in the corner. Strangers holding hands and gazing lovingly into one another's eyes, their drinks unheeded. Not strangers to Markham, however. Two police officers, chosen for their similar ages, who may not have known each other before that evening but who were doing a good job of appearing moonstruck whilst they watched Petesy French and Mark Howard. They were better than good, he thought, as the girl let out a high-pitched giggle. She did not laugh like that normally. And neither of them had registered his presence, not even by the flickering of an eyelid.

'Can I have a word, Tony?'

'Again?' Tony Peak was a massive man. Not quite as tall as the Chief, but almost, and he must have weighed eighteen stone or more. His blue and white striped shirt was open half-way down his chest revealing a mat of black hair which matched that on his forearms. The mass of his stomach concealed his belt which held up shiny blue serge trousers. Longish black hair curled around his collar and heavy eyebrows and a bushy beard concealed most of his face. What skin was visible was brick red and heavily veined.

'Yes. Again.'

'So you couldn't nail Petesy then? Can't believe you thought he'd done it.'

Markham did not respond. His hands were in the pockets of his leather jacket; his cold blue eyes stared unblinkingly at Peak.

'All right. Upstairs, though.'

Upstairs? It was the first time Markham had been granted the privilege. Peak obviously didn't have anything to hide. Or, with a murder investigation under way, one which had included the arrest of one of his customers, he'd made damn sure there was nothing to find. It was a risk. Markham did not want to appear to be fraternising with the landlord.

'Carol? Look after the bar, would you? I've got a visitor,' Peak shouted out to the kitchen area. In response a short, fat woman hurried out. Circles of sweat stained the armpits of the cotton blouse over which she wore an apron showing the tell-tale signs of cooking. On her feet were flip-flops. Brushing back lank, mousy hair, she sighed in exasperation. 'Don't I ever get a minute's peace? Oh.' She stopped. Recognising Markham, she managed a weak smile. Knowing the hours her husband kept, she was not about to upset the police. 'Do you want some coffee sent up?'

'No thanks.' Markham followed the huge man up the stairs and was surprised at the living accommodation, which was in direct contrast to the pub below. A light spacious lounge looked out over the street and the plane trees which lined it. The furniture was modern but not tatty. The three-piece suite was a creamy colour with little flecks of brown and tan and sat well on the light brown carpet which matched the curtains. There was a glass-topped coffee table on which stood only a clean crystal ashtray. Standards may not be high downstairs but a lot of effort was made up here.

'How come you were so certain it wasn't Petesy?'

Tony shrugged expansively then sat down with a grunt, his shirt buttons straining dangerously. 'Just couldn't see it. I mean, where would a toe-rag like that get a gun anyhow?'

'I know you've already been questioned but this is important. Before I start I want you to know that at the moment your opening hours don't concern us, OK? Nor will they be brought into this case.'

Tony nodded, feeling a great sense of relief. He'd had his suspicions that the police were on to him.

'So tell me again about yesterday.'

'Take the weight off them.' Tony indicated one of the armchairs. A spotless white net curtain stirred in the slight breeze coming through the window. They both turned to look at it. It was the first stirring of air for many days. 'I came down and did the cleaning, like I always do weekdays, Carol does weekends, then I stocked up the bar and put on another barrel of lager.' There was no real ale in the place which was one of the reasons why the Chief refused to use it. 'The usual crowd started drifting in.' He paused, still uncertain about

Markham's promise. 'It was about ten forty, something like that. Petesy was here just before eleven. I remember that because he said something like only three hours and a few minutes and I'll be a rich man. He was waving a betting slip about. Mind you, he usually is at that time of day.'

'Good.' That cleared up the missing fifteen or so minutes. 'Who else was here?'

'I told you before.'

'I know. But in view of the fact that you also told me your first customers arrived yesterday at various times after eleven I thought your memory might have improved.'

'Yes, well, point taken. Let me see. Mark Howard, Petesy, Danny Matthews, George the Post, he always stops for one on his way home after his round. Bilton-Jones and Fry, a couple I've never seen before and the old boy with his dog. That's all I can remember up to about twelve thirty. After that we get the lunchtime crowd, the ones who sip a mineral water and eat. It was too busy to take a lot of notice then. Still, there's money to be made in food these days.

'After two it quietens down again. People back at work, some of the lads down the betting shop checking their horses. They come back on and off, but it's stragglers mainly until five.'

'And French?'

'He was here until about twelve thirty. About, I say, because I can't be more accurate than that. You could have a word with Carol but she would've been in the kitchen or in and out with the food, I doubt if she'd have noticed anything.' The sweat had dried on Tony's brow as the temperature quickly dropped.

'Odd that. Petesy can hold his drink, small as he is. I do remember that when he went out to the Gents he was swaying a bit. I was going to send someone out to see if he was all right, he'd been a long time, see, when he came back. Said something about tripping down the step. Anyway, he left right after that. Went out the door and turned left, took his bag with him. And that's it.'

'And he definitely left alone?'

'Yes, I'm positive.'

'Anyone leave soon after?'

'No. Well, not that soon. Like I keep saying, I'm not their minder.'

'Thanks, Tony.' Markham stood up, a frown of concentration on his face. 'Bilton-Jones and his sidekick, they come in here regularly. What's the appeal, do you think?'

Tony Peak glanced towards the window, avoiding Markham's fixed gaze. 'You know what it's like, a man with all that dough, he likes slumming it and he likes people to see he can afford his own driver. He's not such a bad sort once you get to know him.'

Markham nodded and went to the door. Tony Peak remained in his chair.

'Sorry, I'll show you down.'

'No need, I can find the way.'

He re-entered the bar and walked straight through it out into the street without looking at any of the customers. Something's not right, he thought as he headed back to the station. And whatever it was he didn't necessarily think it was to do with Petesy French.

'What's all this then? This thing with the ABH?' Brenda studied DC Campbell's profile as he drove out of the town. As she had known it would do, his skin reddened. He blushed easily.

'Just a feeling.'

She folded her arms. Alan was responsible and dedicated and double-checked things to such an extent he was almost obsessional. But a feeling about a case, or cases? Most unusual. She wouldn't press him. The chances were that he was wrong and she didn't want to make a fool of him.

They pulled into the Goodwins' drive and parked next to a shiny red hatchback to one side of the terrace. There was no sign of life and the shutters were drawn across one pair of french windows.

The heat was oppressive, like a physical weight pressing down on their heads, and the sky was a blinding white, tinged with yellow on the horizon. Brenda's skirt stuck to her and her shirt felt grubby although it was clean that morning. She was not suffering alone. Alan's shirt was damp between his shoulder blades and the faint sheen on his pallid face made him look ill. His permanent unhealthy appearance was deceptive: he had never been known to take a day off sick.

A short, scrawny woman answered Brenda's sharp rap with the knocker. Badly dyed hair frizzed around her face and her eyes were puffy with crying.

'We're police officers. Rickenham Green CID.' Automatically they produced their identification. 'Are Mr and Mrs Goodwin at home?'

'Ay, and the daughter. Flora.' The last word was added quickly, with a catch in her voice as tears filled her eyes. She wiped them with a handkerchief which had been balled up in her hand. 'Come in,' she said and they followed her silently down the wide hallway; the only sound was the clicking of Brenda's heels on the black and white chequered floor. Ahead was a wide staircase beside which, on the left-hand side, ran a narrower passageway leading to the kitchen and laundry room. On either side of them were heavy wooden doors, all closed. The woman tapped on one and opened it without waiting for an answer. 'It's the police,' she said, standing aside to let them pass.

'Thank you, Mrs Maddern.' An elegant woman, seated in a high-backed chair, had spoken. She must once have been beautiful but now there was raw grief in her face. A younger woman sat at her feet, black hair gleaming, her lips bright red and pursed as she squinted to light a cigarette. She had smoked a lot, the ashtray was almost full. But she was dry-eyed and did not appear to have shed a tear. Erica and Flora Goodwin. Completing the cameo, which might have formed a family portrait, was Cliff Goodwin who stood beside his wife's chair, one hand resting on her shoulder. When Brenda and Alan entered the room he moved away and stood with his back to the mantelpiece, his hands in the pockets of his lightweight trousers. He nodded, as if to say they had been expecting this intrusion into their grief but that he understood the reason for it.

Brenda made the introductions again.

'Your colleagues were very kind yesterday. They more than did their duty as far as we were concerned. Will you pass on our thanks?' Cliff Goodwin said.

'Of course.' That would be Judy Robbins. Always the best when it came to situations like this. She had no set way of doing things and often what she said came out wrong, but she behaved so naturally it always put people at ease. Brenda decided they had no option but to tread carefully despite the aggressive way in which Flora Goodwin was glaring at her.

'We've spoken to Joff. We asked him to come and stay,' Erica Goodwin said. 'We thought it might help us all come to terms with it, but he refused. He sounded absolutely dreadful. He said he couldn't bear to be here, where there are so many reminders of Jassy's childhood.' She paused. Brenda and Alan guessed at the unspoken words. If Joff felt that way, how much harder for her parents who had brought her up here. Erica pressed her lips together tightly. Speaking her daughter's name still brought tears and she knew it would continue to do so for some time.

'He's staying with one of our colleagues, he's in good hands,' Alan said quietly, hoping to offer some reassurance.

'I'm glad.' Erica smiled.

'I hear you got the wrong man.' Flora, long legs stretched out in front of her, remained sitting on the floor, studying the end of her cigarette. When there was no response she looked up and met Brenda's expressionless but unyielding gaze before looking away quickly, thinking how unfair it was that a policewoman could look so stunning without even a trace of make-up when she, Flora, spent hours making herself look presentable. She had always had to try so hard to create an effect, to be noticed. It had been the same all her life. She might have been the older sister but she was always the underdog. Even now Jassy was the centre of attention. It was a mean and wicked thought and Flora knew it but she had hoped, just for once, that her parents could have shown some gratitude, or at least gained comfort from the fact that she had come home immediately, leaving the magazine in the lurch.

'We need to ask you a few questions,' Brenda continued as if she had not been interrupted. 'We need to know as much as possible about your daughter and the people she knew. If it's not convenient, or if it's too much for you to cope with at the moment, we can come back.'

'No.' Cliff Goodwin sat down and invited Alan and Brenda to do the same. 'The sooner we get this over with, the better. I have to admit, we were bitterly disappointed when we rang earlier and were told that the man you suspected had been released. Please, go ahead. We'll try our best to answer your questions.'

The next twenty minutes or so were spent going over Jassy's background: her schooling, her hobbies, her friends and, lastly, her marriage.

Alan caught Brenda's eye in much the same way that Erica and Cliff exchanged a glance when they spoke of Joff. With a small nod Brenda indicated that they would come back to that later.

'She always kept in touch with her friends, even when she went to Paris. From her letters and what she said when she returned, we gathered she didn't make any new ones there, which was disappointing. The whole idea was to widen her horizons. She always was a good correspondent, though. To be honest, I don't think she enjoyed her sojourn abroad, although, at the time, we thought it would be good for her. She spent too much time here with us, you see. I wish now that we hadn't insisted. We could have had that extra year with her.' Erica sniffed but held the tears at bay.

Flora lifted her face to her mother's. There was pain in her eyes. She spoke softly and quietly. 'You didn't force her to go.'

'No, darling, we didn't exactly force her.' She turned back to Brenda. 'Jasmine was always so accommodating. Cliff and I have often said we think she was born in the wrong century. Not many girls her age were content to stay at home without a career and she did all the things most young women consider to be old-fashioned, like writing letters and sewing. And she read a great deal. I can't recall seeing her without a book to hand. When she got married she threw herself into it. She was determined to have a lovely home with everything just so. She doesn't get that from me, I don't know where we'd be without Mrs Maddern. And there were her groups and causes. Jassy was a great organiser.' Erica sighed. 'So very unalike, our two daughters. I shouldn't say this, but it's not something Jassy didn't know – I always expected more of her, somehow. I kept thinking she was wasting her life.'

'In what way?' Alan Campbell took over. 'By getting married young?'

'Oh, no, she seemed to idolise Joff, and he her.' There was another pause as if a 'but' had quickly been omitted. 'She couldn't have found a man who treated her better. No, I meant for herself, intellectually, I suppose. She could have got into university if she'd tried, she could have used her life. You see, I always felt she lacked a challenge, that life was too easy. But she had a good marriage and all my hopes don't mean a damn when you see what's happened to her. I'm glad now that she did have it easy.'

'I think she was very happy with Joff.' Alan blushed, knowing he should not be making personal comments in a situation which included a murder victim and one of his fellow officers. However, no one seemed to have heard him.

'I've always worked,' Erica continued. 'I always found I needed some sort of stimulation. I still do. I organise educational trips these days, for foreign students. Anyway, when Flora put her foot down and said she had no intention of wasting a year abroad I was so pleased. At least she knew at an early age what she didn't want.'

Erica smiled down at her surviving child. Flora's mouth was slightly open. She shook her head in confusion.

'And then when she took herself off to London and found a flat and a job, one in which she excels, I can't tell you how proud we were. It was only then I felt we hadn't gone so badly wrong if one of our daughters was such a success. Well, you've only got to look at her.'

Brenda was about to bring her back to the point but stopped herself. Gone badly wrong? What had Mrs Goodwin meant by that? Maybe it was better to let her talk. Meanwhile myriad expressions were crossing Flora's face, from horror to disbelief and other indefinable things. Finally her eyes filled with tears and they ran down her face, unchecked, leaving a snail's trail through the make-up.

Flora Goodwin had never known how her parents felt and had spent most of her life being jealous of her sister. But had she been overshadowed enough to kill her or have her killed? It was not beyond the bounds of possibility. Flora's alibi might check out but she was earning enough to have the job done. It was amazing how cheap it could be to arrange for a killing: a few thousand pounds, sometimes less.

'Oh, Mum!'

'I say.' Cliff Goodwin had to move quickly. He was in Flora's direct line as she jumped to her feet and threw herself into her mother's arms.

So she does have feelings, Brenda thought, nowhere near as embarrassed as Alan Campbell at the emotional tableau taking place in front of them. Could all this emotion be due to guilt? Had Flora somehow rid herself of her sister only to discover that there had been no need?

No one was sure what to say. Brenda was about to get back to her questions when, on cue, Mrs Maddern opened the door and came in wheeling a trolley. Brenda wondered if she had been listening outside. Her appearance settled everyone down. Flora now took a seat and lit another cigarette.

The trolley contained a pot of coffee and cups and saucers and an array of drinks and glasses on the lower shelf. Mrs Maddern made no comment as she turned and left the room.

The sun had dropped below the horizon and Brenda shivered as a sudden draught swept through the terrace windows and across the room. It was a very long time since she had felt chilly. At last the weather was breaking. She hoped that the same would apply to the case. The garden was in shadow. A hosepipe trailed across the lawn, left there from the previous evening when Cliff had been about to water the borders, but the police had come with the news instead.

'Mrs Goodwin, can we talk some more about Jasmine?' Alan had accepted a cup of coffee and now took the initiative. Only Flora mixed herself an alcoholic drink.

'Of course. I'm sorry, I didn't mean to side-track you.'

'Did you see a lot of Jasmine after she was married?'

'She came here at least once a week, mostly more frequently. Sometimes she stayed all day. If I went into Rickenham I sometimes called in. But this last month, come to think of it, her visits weren't quite as regular.'

'Have you any idea why this might be?'

'No. It really hadn't occurred to me until you asked.'

'Do you think she might have been worried about something?'

Erica thought about it and shook her head. 'No. Not worried. We spoke on the telephone most days. Yes, now you mention it, once or twice I did think she sounded a bit vague, but not worried, I wouldn't go as far as to say that. If something was troubling her she didn't confide in me.'

Cliff Goodwin interrupted. 'I'm sure Jassy would have done so. They were very close. More like friends than mother and daughter. We tried to discourage her, tactfully, from coming home so much. We felt it ought to be Joff who was her confidant. Perhaps our endeavours were beginning to be successful.'

Alan nodded. That might be the explanation, but how

much better it would be if there was a different reason, one which would lead them closer to their target. It was not to be found here among the Goodwins, however.

Brenda placed her cup and saucer on the table beside her. 'Did Joff visit often?' She looked up just in time to catch the quick look which passed between Jassy's parents.

'No. He was always at work when Jassy came here, she rarely came over in the evenings.' Erica toyed with the buttons on her cotton dress then, like a child reprimanded for fidgeting, clasped her hands neatly in her lap. 'How's Sally Foster? That poor girl, what a shock it must have been for her.'

'She's coping.'

Brenda let Alan continue. Although they were the same rank she often felt his superior, a fact which, if he noticed, caused him no offence.

'I wonder . . .' All heads turned to Flora who seemed not to have been listening. 'I think there may have been something on her mind. We spoke on the phone now and then, we weren't close, not like some sisters, our lifestyles have always been too different for much intimacy, but we'd have a chat, about what she'd been doing to the house or the drama productions, and I'm sure I probably bored her with my talk of work. But last week, I think it was Monday, she rang up and I wondered why she'd bothered. She didn't say much, I did most of the talking, but I got the impression she wasn't really listening, or taking it in. She told me that Joff was going away for a few days so I put it down to that. They spent every free minute together, you see.'

'It's true,' Erica added. 'He went to all her drama productions.'

'But she didn't actually say anything to give you cause for alarm?' The question was addressed to Flora.

'No. Perhaps because of the circumstances, I'm reading more into it than there was. I just had the feeling that there was something she wanted to say to me. God, how I wish now I'd asked.'

The past twenty-four hours had been spent concentrating on Jassy's side of the family. People on Joff's side would also need to be investigated. Having received the Goodwins' list of their daughter's friends, Brenda and Alan left.

'What do you make of it? Did you get the impression there were things left unsaid?'

Alan got into the driver's seat. 'Yes, I did.' He had seen the quickly exchanged glance between the senior Goodwins.

'Perhaps there was some friction. I mean, it seems Joff doesn't visit much. Perhaps they don't like him.'

Alan shrugged. 'In-laws. It's often the case.'

'Yep. Maybe. Come on, let's go. I'm going out tonight.'

'Andrew?'

'Yes.'

'I like him.'

'You do?' Brenda was surprised. She had not realised that Alan knew him well enough to express an opinion. Of course, they were often in the pub at the same time and although Alan said little there was nothing wrong with his hearing.

In true British fashion many conversations revolved around the weather that Friday morning. As the night had lengthened the temperature had dropped further. A strong wind rose and then abated suddenly, creating a strange stillness which was finally broken by thunder. It crashed overhead for almost an hour and lightning zigzagged in flashes of white, briefly illuminating the world like daylight. The downpour which came with it continued ceaselessly and water ran straight off the hard-baked fields and flooded the roads. It overflowed from gutters and joined the gurgling streams running along the kerb.

The morning dawned grey and damp, trees dripped and litter was sodden. Everyone everywhere said how much the rain was needed and what good it would do to their gardens. Even Moira, who eschewed small talk of this kind, said it would save her getting out the watering can.

DCI Roper swore as he ran up the steps to the station. One of his shoes leaked and his sock was soaking. DS Barry Swan was loitering in the reception area looking as if he hadn't slept.

'What're you doing in so early?'

'I thought it might be quieter here. That boy's got one hell of a pair of lungs on him.'

'There'll be a lot more of that.' Ian knew that Lucy's parents would be around to ease the burden. 'Well, you might as well team up with DC Hanson. Three cases of ABH now. There was another one.'

'Motiveless again?'

'Harder to tell this time. The victim's a Pakistani but no one except Sadiqi seems to think it was race-induced.'

Barry had hoped to be included in the murder inquiry but he was aware that everyone already had their appointed tasks and at this stage he would be more of a hindrance than a help.

'Oh, how's the family? Apart from the screaming?'

'Mother and baby are fine, as they say. He's called Martin, by the way. Martin Ian.'

Ian's look of surprise was gratifying. He smiled, forgetting his wet foot, and rested his hand on the shorter man's shoulder. 'That's nice. Thanks. Come on then. Briefing time.'

There was not much briefing to be done. Number three squad's efforts had proved fruitless: the rota of officers keeping tabs on Petesy French reported that he had remained in the pub until ten then gone back to his digs and was still there when the shift changed. Brenda and Alan had reported back the previous evening but, apart from their own speculations, could reveal nothing new. Markham's interview with Tony Peak hadn't taken them any further forward but he was certain that Peak wasn't lying when he said he knew of no one who drank in his pub, or anyone anywhere, for that matter, who was involved in firearms. It seemed impossible not to have any leads. Usually there were at least some to start with, even if they went nowhere. At this stage anything would be welcome.

Singly and in pairs they left the general office. DCI Roper went to his own office. There was one thing he wanted to double-check. He picked up the telephone and dialled an outside line.

Barry Swan went to join DC Hanson. Craig Hanson was more commonly known as Crab, which was not a reflection upon his temperament but upon the way he moved. Of medium height but angular, he appeared to sidle through the corridors, bony elbows jutting awkwardly. He had a snub nose and soft brown hair which made him appear younger than his thirty-five years. If anyone was asked whether they liked him they would look surprised. Of course they did. But afterwards they would realise that they hardly knew him. It was a rare occurrence if he joined them at the pub because he claimed he was a family man, preferring to spend time with his wife and two small children rather than socialising elsewhere. This was a lie. As a detective he was average, never doing anything which might lead the way to promotion but always doing enough to ensure his job was safe. Craig Hanson wasn't lazy but nor was he ambitious. He took life as it came.

Barry Swan opened the door of the room DC Hanson was using to co-ordinate the details of the ABH cases. Bending over the table was the Crab. His first view of the crustacean-like figure was of his legs and backside as he bent over the table, head in hands, studying something in his long-sighted manner.

'Sorry, sarge, I didn't hear you come in.'

'It's OK.'

'How's the baby?'

'He's fine. The Chief's said I'm to join you.'

'Good. Do you want . . .?' Hanson was holding out a file but Barry shook his head immediately.

'No, just tell me.' He hadn't been in at the start; it would be easier to have a general idea and the Crab's opinions first, before he read through the statements.

'Another one Wednesday night. Sometime after 10 p.m. One David Sadiqi. Beaten up badly. He had some of the takings on him.'

'Some?'

'Mm. Seems he puts most of it in the safe behind the shop and takes the rest home with him. He's got the idea that if he's robbed, whichever way, they won't get the lot.'

'Insured?'

'Fully. Has to be. It's an off-licence and video hire outlet.'

'Then why does he bother?' It was a rhetorical question. 'And the others?'

DC Hanson ran through them quickly: Dyfan Roberts, aged fifty-two, owner of the London Hotel, and Tony Gregson of the Convenience Store which served the council estate to the north of the town.

'Business good?'

'He says so. His profit margin's high but he keeps long hours and makes his money on goods people run out of or have forgotten at the supermarket. Why?'

'My nasty suspicious mind. I just thought he might have arranged it so's he could claim from the Criminal Injuries Compensation Board.'

'Nah. He wouldn't get enough to justify it. Couple of thou, maybe?'

'And now Sadiqi. Bit of a coincidence, wouldn't you say? All three running their own business?'

'Not necessarily. All three were attacked at roughly the same time, between ten and ten thirty. Sadiqi was on his way home, as was Gregson. It's a lock-up. And Roberts, who lives at the London Hotel, was popping down the road for a pint. He said he gets fed up with making small talk to the guests.'

'OK, so it could be a couple of blokes with a vicious bent, too many drinks, perhaps, and they pick on a single man, minding his own business, and give him a good hiding.'

'That's the way we're looking at it, sarge. We've stepped up patrol cars between nine and eleven thirty.'

Barry nodded and strolled to the large map of Rickenham Green which was pinned to the wall.

'I put that up this morning. Two attacks? Well, it happens. Coincidence. But three seems to be the start of a pattern. If we don't get 'em, there might be more and I thought it'd be helpful to mark the areas.'

'Mm.' Barry glanced at the three pins with their red plastic heads. They formed a rough triangle which might or might not be relevant. What was relevant was that each man had been attacked minutes after leaving his premises, which suggested that the perpetrators were local and knew the habits of the victims. He put the theory to Hanson.

'We've looked at that angle. Fine in the case of Gregson and Sadiqi but Roberts's life follows no routine. Once or twice a week he goes out for what he calls a nightcap. Different pubs, different routes but, more importantly, it's rarely the same two nights.'

'And the interviews with the victims?'

Hanson shrugged, elbows lifted, before making his ungainly way to a table in front of the window. The rain, which had started again, splattered against it as the rising wind swept it along the street. Outside people held umbrellas in front of their faces and battled along like so many forward-leaning Mary Poppinses. The sky was leaden, more reminiscent of a winter afternoon than nine o'clock on a summer Friday morning. Overhead the fluorescent light flickered. Barry and Craig looked at it and waited silently for several seconds. It remained on. There had been a power cut in the night when lines had been damaged by the storm. Barry had noticed because it had occurred in the early hours just as his son had made his hunger known. Craig was aware of it because the clock on his electric cooker had shown five thirty when his watch told him it was three minutes past six.

'Another coincidence?' Barry inquired when he had read through the brief statements obtained from the victims.

'Sarge?'

'None of them know of anyone who wished them harm, held a grudge or anything similar.'

'Well, that makes sense if they're random attacks.'

'Do you think they are? Or do you think perhaps they're not saying?'

'What else can they be?'

'Two assailants in the first two incidents, only one in Sadiqi's case. Could this be why?' Barry slung some photographs on to the table. They fanned out like playing cards. Each showed the head and torso of one of the victims, the parts that received injuries. They would be used in evidence if a case came to court. 'See? Sadiqi's a much smaller man than the other two. You can tell, even from these.'

Hanson nodded in agreement, hoping his embarrassment didn't show. It was certainly a factor. Sadiqi's frame was small, almost childlike. His pale brown skin stretched tautly over his ribs.

'Can't tell for certain, but I'd guess he's no more than – what, five five, five six?'

'All right, so it wouldn't take two men to overpower him. But how would they know he wasn't into martial arts or something?'

'Good question. A man like Sadiqi, though? You know the hours his shop keeps. Even if he isn't there all the time, he'd have little time for recreation.'

'You think the victims are hiding something? I can't see it myself. There's no connection between them.'

'None that we know of yet, and that's what we're going to find out.'

'Strange thing, Campbell said much the same thing.' Hanson sat down and leaned on the table, with the photographs still in his hand.

'Campbell did?'

'Surprised me a bit too.' Hanson laughed; it was a low and pleasant sound and held more affection than derision. The two men were dissimilar in many ways but they shared a preference for keeping their private lives separate from the job. 'He said there was something he was going to look into if he had the time.'

'Like what?'

'He didn't go so far as to say.'

Barry did not like the sound of that. Campbell had been taken off these cases – any information or even ideas that he held should be shared or passed on. It was dangerous, stupid and not what he was being paid to do.

Barry joined Hanson at the table, ready to read through the statements. All three men had initially been interviewed in their hospital beds. Painful interviews through swollen lips, breathing difficult because of cracked ribs. These reports told him nothing. Tony Gregson had been seen again once he had been discharged and was back at home, likewise Roberts. 'Hmm.'

'Sarge?'

'Notice anything else about these attacks?'

'Yes, now you mention it. Coincidence number four? The injuries are very similar, enough to put them in hospital for a night or two but nothing to cause permanent damage.'

'Which suggests . . .' Barry's head was on one side as he waited for an answer.

'That unless it's pure chance, someone knew exactly what he was doing.'

'Exactly.' Hanson might not be destined to be one of the best but he was not slow on the uptake.

'Oh, my God. Professionals?'

'Could be. Which begs the question, why?'

Hanson nodded. There could only be one possible explanation, taking all the facts into account. Or two. But they both amounted to the same thing. 'I think we ought to concentrate on the similarities, dig a bit deeper into their lives.'

'That's where Alan's so good.'

'Yes, but Alan's otherwise engaged. Come on, get your coat.'

Barry looked out of the window but the rain was in for the

day. For almost an hour his mind had been on work. He could hardly believe Lucy and Martin had taken a back seat already. Fine. He knew the dangers. Of course he must concentrate whilst he was on duty but he would not allow any neglect to creep into his home life. He had seen too often what it did to a marriage.

Before they reached the revolving glass doors at the front of the building both men stopped to button their raincoats. Together they ran across the car-park and signed for one of the pool cars. Without hesitation Barry got behind the wheel. He always drove unless someone else insisted upon doing so.

'We'll take them in reverse order.'

'Any particular reason?' Hanson inquired as he disentangled himself from the seat belt which he had managed to twist and get caught up in.

'It might be, on our reappearance, that Sadiqi or Roberts thinks that the first victim has said more than he ought.'

'You're presupposing we're right.'

'We?' Barry looked across and grinned.

'Sorry, sarge. You.'

'Thank you.' He smoothed back his hair over the spot where his pink scalp tended to show through. It was so much a habit of his that no one noticed any more, and although he still retained a stylish manner of dressing he was nowhere near as vain as he once had been.

Hanson sat, arms folded, aware that his own well-worn jeans, the checked shirt and V-necked lightweight sweater were no match for Barry's sharply creased moss green trousers, his crisp white shirt and the subtle tie fastened in a complicated knot which Hanson had never been successful in contriving. Their macs were on the back seat. Hanson grinned. It might be that DS Swan succeeded in walking up the High Street, or wherever, in weather like this without getting dirty splashes on the back of his legs, but it was doubtful he'd avoid puke down his back when it was his turn to wind the baby. It was a gratifying thought.

Sadiqi had been discharged that morning. His wife had

111

collected him, having taken the children to her sister's. 'The business must be doing well.' Hanson nodded towards the house as they surveyed it for a minute or so from the dryness of the car.

Barry leant over. To his left was a pebble-dashed semi-detached property. The paintwork looked fresh although not recently new, the small front garden was neat and there was an Audi parked in the open garage. Nets hung at all the windows. They were pink. Each to his own, Barry thought. He hated any sort of net curtain.

Mrs Sadiqi opened the door. Unlike her husband she was dressed colourfully in the costume of her country. Her smooth plump arms were encircled by bangles which clinked as she moved. She was still pretty but hers was the build which would later turn to fat.

The two men introduced themselves. Mrs Sadiqi's English was good although she used the phraseology of her own tongue. With a small inclination of her head she showed them into the living-room where her husband sat in a corner of the settee with a pillow from one of the beds behind him. He started to get up, groaned, and thought better of it just as DS Swan raised a hand to let him know there was no need to move.

'I thought someone would come. Thank you. Please, be seated.' He glanced to one side. His wife stood hesitantly in the doorway, unsure if she was expected to stay or go. David Sadiqi spoke to her in a language his visitors were unable to understand. She nodded and walked quietly from the room, closing the door behind her with hardly a sound. 'I do not wish my wife to be more upset.'

'We might need to speak to her at some point,' Barry said. 'Mr Sadiqi, one of our constables has already asked you some questions. Obviously he did not wish to distress you whilst you were in pain, but now we need more details. Are you feeling better?'

'Ah, yes, sir. Much, much better. My brother is kindly keeping the shop.' He raised a hand to stem any protest, but none was forthcoming. 'It is all in order. I have checked with the authorities.'

They could only guess that he meant something to do with the licensing laws, over which Sadiqi seemed a little confused.

'It is a bad time to happen. We have a flight for Peshawar where we were to join our families. We had hoped, this year, to go on, to Mecca, to make the great *hajj*, our pilgrimage. It is the festival of Dhu'l-Hijja, you see.'

Barry and Craig nodded wisely as if they were fully *au fait* with pilgrimages and Mecca. 'But you're not going?'

Mr Sadiqi spread his arms expansively which caused him to groan again. 'I do not know that it is safe. How can I leave my brother in charge? What if the same thing happens to him?'

'Do you think it might?'

'It is possible. It is sad to say that some people do not realise we are British citizens. Here, it is good. My sons have no trouble at school, but then, children can be far more tolerant than adults if there is nothing to influence them otherwise. Later, who knows? They will move away, get jobs. Ah, but it is no use worrying about the future.'

'When you spoke to Constable Potter you suggested . . .' Barry paused to look at the notebook in his hand. Not because he needed reminding but because he felt embarrassed at bringing it up. The harder he tried not to, the more racist he was sure he sounded. 'That the attack might have been to do with the colour of your skin. I believe they were your words.'

'Indeed. What else can I think? I have harmed no one, I have done nothing illegal, nor has any member of my family. We do not give credit, therefore I have not had to ask anyone for money which maybe a customer does not have. You tell me, Detective Swan, just what else can I think?' Sadiqi seemed to slump in his chair, as if, at long last, his worst fears had come true.

'The man who attacked you – you have had some time to think about it. Is there anything about him which you can recall? It does not matter how small the detail.' Barry coughed. Stop it, he told himself. He was almost imitating the man's formal manner of speech. He turned around. The door had opened and Mrs Sadiqi came in pushing a gilt trolley. On it were cups and saucers and a steaming pot of tea. Arranged on a plate were what looked like small cakes. The interruption had come at the right time. It allowed Barry to realise that it was better not to try too hard, but just to treat the victim normally. Of course, if Sadiqi was right it might prove that there was no connection between the three crimes.

It was Mrs Sadiqi who took up the conversation as she handed them each a cup and a plate. 'We had hoped to avoid this sort of thing. It is very sad. We mean no one harm. We are of the Islam faith and we keep our five pillars of faith.'

'Thank you.' Barry accepted the tea and the plate. Was this talk of religion and racism a distraction or were these the good people he felt them to be? He bit into the sticky square. It tasted of coconut and something else and was sickly sweet. No wonder it was so small. The Sadiqis smiled as each man ate; Barry hoped that this was because accepting the food was the polite thing to do.

'My husband does not know the man. He told me that.' The statement implied that David Sadiqi would not have lied.

'I did not even see him. I was walking home. From behind I felt an arm around my neck and someone was punching me in the back. I tripped and covered my face with my arms but he was kicking me. Soon I heard his footsteps as he ran away. I did not look up. You must think me a coward but I believed that if he saw me looking at him he might come back and hurt me more. I was too weak then to struggle and I think anyway I could not have hit the man.'

'Nothing you can remember? Aftershave? The colour of his shoes? Was he wearing jeans?'

'Yes. Jeans. And boots. Brown leather with laces.'

Barry sighed inwardly. That narrows it down, he thought wryly. 'Could you guess at his age?'

'No. He did not speak. He did not utter one word. I

114

thought he would ask me for money or my watch.' Sadiqi held out his wrist. The strap of the watch was constructed with heavy gold links. 'I waited until I felt stronger but a couple came along and took me to the hospital. You see, I did not want to go there really but I did not want to come home in case they followed me.'

'They?' It was Craig Hanson who picked this up.

'Forgive me. A figure of speech. There was only one man. At the time I thought he might have someone waiting for him, in case I was too strong for him.'

'Just one more thing, Mr Sadiqi, and we'll leave you in peace. Had you received any threats of any kind, prior to the attack, that is?'

'Threats? Who would wish to threaten me? I have done no harm.'

'It was just a thought.' Barry smiled and placed his plate on the trolley, taking in the room as he did so. The furnishings were middle range in price, he estimated, and everything was very clean, although he found the choice of colours a little bright. That was not the point – what was, was that this house had all the appearances of being that of a hard-working family man who would, if such things occurred to him, call himself middle-class. He was by no means poor but neither was he massively wealthy. Why, then, was he so frightened? At the mention of the word 'threats' his voice had risen an octave in replying. Barry would not push them now, not until he had spoken to Dyfan Roberts.

'I hope your injuries heal quickly.' Barry stood and Hanson followed his lead.

'You are very kind.'

Mrs Sadiqi showed them to the door. 'He must rest now,' was all she said before shutting it, again almost soundlessly, behind them.

The rain had eased, but not by much. Neither man had bothered to wear his raincoat for the few short yards to the front door. They sat in the front of the car. 'He's scared.' They spoke in unison.

'Too scared to talk,' Hanson continued. 'All the time I was watching his eyes. It showed.'

Barry nodded as he turned the key in the ignition. 'Protecting his family, most likely. If whoever it was knows him, he'll know where he lives. A man like that, one who cares for his family, he'd probably do anything rather than endanger them.'

'Including lying to us.'

'I'm not so sure he considers it to be lying. I'm not sure – is it the Indians or the Pakistanis who have no equivalent word in their language? They tell you the truth they think you want to hear and it becomes the truth. Anyway, let's see how we get on with Mr Roberts. What's up?'

Barry was watching his rear view mirror, waiting to pull out, when he heard the Crab's chuckle.

'Odd, you know, I've never minded the Asians. And you can't beat a decent curry.'

'Not you, too. The Chief's bad enough.'

'Can't stand the Welsh though.'

Barry had to laugh at the irony. 'Why not?'

'Don't know. Just can't.'

Barry let it drop. By the way Craig Hanson's face had reddened there had been something in his past he would prefer remained a secret.

7

Spread on his desk were several sheets of paper. They were covered in what appeared, due to the spidery nature of Ian's writing, to be hieroglyphics. The woman at the other end of the telephone had been extremely patient with his requests and had answered them all precisely but in the end he had sent someone down to the railway station to pick up a general timetable. Unbelievably they had not run out. Ian studied the

figures and letters, 'S. 0745 I. 0853 LS. 1000 KC. (FS) 1412 E.'
Next to this first row was a tick. What followed was far more
complicated.

'W. 0600 0610 (7 8 9) then ½ hourly. JT approx 4½ hrs. LS
to I hourly except rush hours when ½ hrly. JT 1hr 5m – 1hr
13m.'

So what? he thought, leaning back in his chair which
creaked beneath his weight. Rain still lashed against the
windows in squally bursts yet the sound was somehow
soothing. Had he thought it worthwhile he would have made
a list of what they had and another of what they needed to
know. Lists were the way in which he put his thoughts into
order. But what did they have? No sexual motive, no theft –
although that could not be discounted entirely, whoever it
was may have panicked – no apparent grudges. Jealousy?
Maybe on the sister's part, but enough to kill? Ian doubted it.
Why should a woman who lived a successful life in the
capital take it into her head to rush home and do her sister
in? Flora's salary was not far off the top bracket and the
Goodwins' joint wills split everything between their daughters. Unless Flora was remarkably greedy and coveted her
sister's share, money was not a motive either.

What of Mrs Maddern, Jeanette Maddern? A faithful
retainer doing her employers what she believed to be a
favour? Now and then it really is the butler, or whatever, Ian
told himself. Except Mrs Maddern had been with the Goodwins from 9.30 a.m. until 4 p.m. and she had come across as
an honest women, genuinely distressed by Jassy's death.

'Oh, for Christ's sake!' he said, loudly enough that someone passing in the corridor paused outside the door before
moving on again.

Gina came in and handed him a mug of coffee. 'I heard
you in here. I thought this might be welcome.'

'More than you know,' he said gruffly by way of thanks.

Gina went back to her tiny office next door. The clatter of
keys no longer troubled the Chief since she had progressed
to a word processorr. Gina wondered if Jassy had had a

117

jealous lover. She did not know it was the thought uppermost in the minds of everyone who was not involved in the case. She had been so beautiful and she had had plenty of opportunity as she did not go out to work. It hadn't done her much good if that was the case, Gina thought, wishing she could find just one man.

Parents. Ian leant back again, watching the steam rise from the black coffee in front of him. He linked his hands behind his head and stretched. As always he wore his personal uniform of grey trousers, a white shirt – Moira sent his shirts to the laundry these days – and a checked jacket. Not the tweedy one similar to one his own father had worn, but a smart black and white dog-tooth or a tan with a thin red check which Moira had assured him was both fashionable and suitable. Because he loathed shopping he had accepted her word and bought them in the first shop they had entered. Now he rather liked them.

Parents. He was drifting again and he knew it was because, however hard he tried, he would not be able to come up with a reason why the Goodwins should want their married daughter dead. He had to remind himself that just because he couldn't come up with a reason did not mean there wasn't one. Tennis club, Drama Guild, old school friends, all these people who had known her and who, seemingly, had nothing to hide and nothing to gain from her death. The girl at the club: he had to check the name. Philippa Jackson. He understood that sort of relationship. One girl plain, one pretty, the plain girl putting up with whatever was dished out because she needed to be included in the glow which surrounded her friend. Not friends, but not enemies either. It was a far more common relationship than people might think. And Ferguson? Had he perhaps made an advance or two and been rebuffed and was therefore using the opportunity to put in a slight dig? That was the problem, everything that they were told could be taken in two ways.

Petesy French? Ah, back to that one. Too bloody obvious, he thought. Someone had shopped him and, he would bet on it, someone had planted the gun, and they had wasted almost twenty-four hours questioning him. He stood up, knocking his chair over behind him.

'Gee-naa!' The Chief's voice reverberated around the corridor. Eyebrows were raised and lips formed smiles as the people in adjoining offices heard the bellow.

She came back into the room at her usual pace, unhurried and unruffled. 'You wanted me?' Ian missed the faint sarcasm.

'Who was the custody officer on Wednesday? Find out. I . . .' He stopped as abruptly as he had begun, holding his head in his hands. 'No. Forget it.' He turned to retrieve his chair, which had dented the cheap waste-paper basket on its way to the floor. No can do, he told himself. It was not the custody officer's fault, it was his, Detective Chief Inspector Roper's fault. The custody officer had acted exactly in the manner in which he should have done. French had been logged in, his belt and the laces from his trainers removed, his possessions listed and signed for; a doctor had been called, as a precaution, in view of the amount of alcohol French had presumably consumed. And the custody officer knew a drunk when he saw one because he had seen hundreds in his time. French was also known to them and that was dangerous. Assumptions tended to be made with known criminals. You knew their form, you knew their aliases, you could almost guarantee where to find them at any given time. French was a hardened drinker with no record of drug abuse and no known associations with dealers or users. No reason then to test for drugs. QED. Except now Ian believed that that was the most likely explanation for his condition. Someone had slipped him something. French's alibi for the time until he left the Black Horse was strong. Everything was as he said it was. The counter staff in the betting shop had sworn he had not been drinking before he arrived to place his bet. He had not. He had done just what he told them he had done. So, whatever had been used to exacerbate the effects of the alcohol could only have been administered in the Black Horse

119

or the toilet of the Black Horse because no one had noticed anything strange about French when he had entered the place.

With a deep sigh, knowing that it was too late for any drugs test to show anything useful now, Ian got out the list of people who had been present at the same time as French, a list which may or may not be complete. For obvious reasons French couldn't remember who was there when he left. Tony Peak, the landlord, had done his best but could not be expected to know the exact times of his customers' comings and goings. His wife, Carol, had been in the kitchen most of the time and more or less everyone else present knew each other and would therefore alibi each other if it was necessary. It was a hopeless task but they would all have to be interviewed again. A stronger line of questioning might jog a few memories.

Two mistakes had been made. Once they knew of the murder, it should have been a priority to find out who rang to say French was in the relevant area. Knowing French's capacity for drink, knowing he had not been in the pub long by his standards and had been sober when he entered it, they, or he, should have put two and two together. They had already suspected that the gun had been planted. If Petesy French had been set up it had been well and truly done. What bothered Ian now was that if what he had surmised held any truth then French was once more a candidate. Yes, they knew him, but under the influence of substances alien to his body they couldn't judge how he might react. Another enigma was how or why he went in the opposite direction from that which he intended. He had his laundry with him, that was a fact, and he had told people he was going to take it to the launderette. The clothes he had been wearing had shown no traces of blood and there were only a few specks on the dirty things in the hold-all, presumably from the gun which may well have been splattered.

'OK. He goes to the pub. Someone puts something in his drink, mightn't be drugs, might be more alcohol. No. The

120

landlord was puzzled by French's drunkenness. If his drink was spiked Peak would have known about it because he served them himself.'

'Sir?' Gina's head appeared around the door.

'Sorry. Thinking aloud.' Ian had been unaware that he was doing so. Gina disappeared with a shake of the head. 'So it has to be drugs. Barbiturates, perhaps. Someone slips the gun into his bag. According to all reports it was at his feet on the floor near the bar where they were all standing. Something is said, some directions given, and Petesy follows them. He staggers out of the pub, goes to the Grants' house and does the deed before collapsing.

Very neat, he thought, getting up and going to the window where he watched the rivulets of water trickle down only to be replaced by others immediately. Neat, yes, but totally illogical. The man would have been incapable of finding his way home let alone anywhere else. French was still under observation. It might be a fatal decision to ignore what common sense was telling him but another point in French's favour was that none of his fingerprints had been found in the house.

Still sifting mentally through the evidence, he made his way down to the canteen. There was a lull in the custom. The lunchtime business was over and it was too early for tea breaks – not that there were set times for these, it all depended upon what was going on, and most officers would swear they missed more than they took.

'Ah, Betty, tea, please and – no, just the tea, I think.'

'Are you sure?' She turned to the urn behind her and added scalding water to a metal teapot already containing a mound of sodden tea-bags, knowing that the Chief preferred it stewed to weak. She smiled to herself as the machine hissed and steam rose around her head. His distorted reflection in the shiny metal of the urn showed that he was still eyeing the tray of bread pudding in front of him. 'Is that it?'

'Yes, thanks.' Ian walked to the end of the counter where Betty ensconced herself behind the till to take his money. The girl whose job this was today was having her own tea break so Betty filled in for fifteen minutes, until the reverse was true. 'There you are, dear.' She handed Ian his change. 'How's it going?'

'Oh, you know . . .'

'Yes, I do.' She had seen that expression before. The Chief often managed to give the impression that everything that was wrong in the world was his personal responsibility. Perhaps he thought it was. How his pretty wife coped was beyond Betty.

It isn't French, it can't be, Ian thought as he slowly stirred the treacle-coloured tea. But it's someone who knows him, someone who knows him well enough to speak to him and to – what? Give him a lift. That's it. Ian nodded emphatically. The time-scale still worked out if he'd walked – but supposing someone had offered to take him home or elsewhere? He'd have probably agreed to it. He got in the car and passed out. The killer did the deed then dumped French near the scene, having first dropped the gun in his bag. That was more like it, a far better scenario, and without the risk of being seen to do so in the pub.

Leaving half the tea he went back upstairs, climbing the first flight to ground level swiftly but having to slow on the flight leading to his office. Five minutes later he tapped out four digits on the internal line and spoke to someone in the incident room. He rattled off the names of the people who had been in the Black Horse between ten thirty and twelve forty-five. 'See them all, bring them in if there're any complaints. Somebody knows something.' It was only when he had organised this and let the controlling officer know what he had done that he saw another possibility. There may have been two people involved; one to doctor his drink, who would remain above suspicion because he or she stayed in the pub, and a second to pick him up outside. He might have intended doing his washing or going home to sleep it off but perhaps someone called out to him, offered him a ride, and, hearing the voice, he turned left instead of right. Well, he could try to find out. Number three squad were at a loose end, they could start in Saxborough Road on the shops nearest to the Black Horse and work their way on to the numerous flat conversions. He had to hope that someone had noticed a fairly drunk man, hold-all in hand, staggering down the road. If they saw him get into a car better still. Please God, he thought. There was nothing more he could do now but wait. Naturally there was the usual pile of forms and papers ready for his signature and, later, Gina would come in with his post. It seemed impossible that each year could bring yet more red tape but it did.

If nothing had been achieved by 6 p.m. he would go home and spend some time with his wife.

DS Barry Swan and DC Hanson called upon Dyfan Roberts. He was in better shape than Sadiqi but he had had longer to recover. There was an interesting selection of bruises on his face, their colours ranging from yellow to black. One eyelid was swollen but there were no sutures and he was able to stand up to greet them when the receptionist showed them in.

Roberts was sitting in the guest lounge; the large television set flickered in the corner but the sound was down low. The room was on the right-hand side of the corridor, the bar to the left of reception. The standard dark red patterned carpet of many such establishments covered the whole of the ground floor and continued on up the stairs. It was a modest hotel which had once been a wool merchant's house. Its six guest bedrooms had been fitted with *en suite* facilities which limited the size of the rooms but Rickenham Green was no tourist resort and businessmen only wanted somewhere to sleep. To keep up with the facilities offered almost everywhere, Roberts had installed small colour TVs in the rooms and a tray with the makings of tea and coffee. The attic had been converted into living accommodation for himself and he had applied for and received planning permission to add a gable window. It was adequate for his needs – his wife had decamped not long after they had taken over the hotel. All this Barry and Craig knew. The backgrounds of the victims had now been thoroughly researched in the hope of finding a connection. There was none, not in their personal or business lives, only the fact that they each ran a business. Roberts's liquor came from a brewery, Sadiqi's from a wholesaler and the Convenience Store was not licensed to sell alcohol. Details as small as these had been gathered and cross-referenced – by DC Alan Campbell needless to say, whose *raison d'être* it was to do such things, and who had volunteered to do it in his own time.

'Can I offer you gentlemen anything?' Roberts asked with every trace of his Swansea origins.

'No thanks.' Barry brushed back his hair, conscious of the hirsuteness of the older man.

'Take a pew, now, why don't you?'

Roberts sank back into his own seat, fumbled down the side of the cushion and retrieved the remote control device then held it out like a weapon. The picture on the television disappeared with a small buzz. 'The other bloke said someone would want to see me again. There's nothing more I can tell you. One of those things, you know? In the wrong place at the wrong time.' Roberts's posture was relaxed. His head was against the back of the chair, his legs crossed at the knee, one foot swinging slightly. Both hands rested on the arms of the chair.

'It's a day or so now, we wondered if anything had come back to you, some small detail.'

'Ah, like in the films, when someone suddenly recalls the attacker wore bright red nail polish? That what you mean?' Roberts laughed. It came from his stomach and startled the other two men by its volume. 'Look, you, I was walking along minding my own business when suddenly, whoomph. I was on the floor. I didn't hear or see anything, not before and not afterwards. I felt it all right, though, I can tell you that. I turned around but it was a slow process and they were running away from me. I was too dizzy to focus right.'

'You saw their backs?' It was Craig Hanson who asked, his pen poised over his notebook.

'I saw their backs and I'll tell you what I told the other one up at Rickenham General. There was nothing about them worth remembering. They could've been any two men. Nondescript clothing, jeans I'm pretty sure, and dark jackets. It was dark, see, so I couldn't even tell you the colour of their hair. All I know is that there were two of them and they were both men.'

'You weren't robbed?'

'No. Perhaps they were scared off. I heard a car and then I saw its headlights, but this was after they'd gone. They'd probably heard it first because they'd have been more alert than me. All I was worrying about right then was my life.'

'Any enemies?'

Roberts frowned and pursed his lips. 'I'm no saint, but I don't think I've got any enemies, at least, no one who'd do that. Believe me, I've given it some thought. It's not like I'm a huge concern, I don't compete with the decent hotels or interfere with the trade of the guest houses. I don't gamble or take drugs. For heaven's sake, man, can't you accept it was a couple of yobbies with nothing better to do with their time?'

Neither officer answered but no, they could not accept it. 'How much do you make out of this place?'

'What?' Roberts was outraged, as he had reason to be. Even Barry, who had asked the question, knew he was going too far. But there was fear beneath his indignation.

'I don't mean to be rude but would you mind telling me if you make a bare living or a comfortable one? You need not be more specific than that.'

'I don't know why you want to know, but I'd say somewhere between the two. Now, that is. When my wife was with me, well, let's just say that there were a lot more personal expenses then than there are now. That's one woman who definitely disproves the saying that two can live as cheaply as one. Now, I've got some bookwork to see to, can I take it that you won't be bothering me again?'

'We'll leave you to it then,' Barry said without answering the question.

Side by side DS Swan and DC Hanson walked down the corridor and out through the half-glass swing doors. The rain had lightened to a drizzle and in the east was a gradually thickening band of light. Steam began to rise from the pavements as the first fingers of sun reached the corner of the hotel car-park where their car was waiting. They arrived at it without speaking, each deep in his own thoughts. 'I'm sure you're right, sarge, and I bet we'll be certain when we've seen Gregson.'

Barry, bent over to unlock the car, straightened up. 'Would you do me a favour, Hanson? Would you stop calling me sarge?'

'Sorry, sir.'

'Jesus! Look, when we're alone Barry will do. OK?'

Craig Hanson ducked his head and slid into the front passenger seat. 'Anything's better than what they call me,' he said.

Barry suppressed a laugh. 'What's the address?'

Hanson replied without having to look it up. He had been on this case from the start, almost ten days now. Gregson was not a pleasant man. He had been interviewed twice already and Hanson wondered how he would take it a third time. No point in warning Swan, he could find out for himself.

The Convenience Store was described in the *Rickenham Herald* as 'your friendly corner shop', according to the advert Gregson paid for spasmodically. Hanson wondered if he could be done under the Trades Descriptions Act. The shop was not on a corner but half-way down a row of red-brick council houses, although it was set back from there by about ten feet with space enough for a couple of cars to park. Over the two front windows were dark green awnings with scalloped edges each bearing the legend 'Convenience Store' and the telephone number, along with the word 'friendly'. He could, Craig thought, probably be done on two counts.

Gregson had tried to widen the range of stock when he had taken the shop over but the specialised ingredients required for the Continental and Asian cooking that people now went in for could be bought more cheaply at the super-markets. He had finally accepted defeat and carried essentials but with a good selection of tinned goods.

He was not behind the counter when Barry and Craig entered. In his stead was a youngish woman, probably in her early thirties but looking tired and careworn. From behind a door came the sound of a wailing child.

They waited whilst she served a customer. There were two others who appeared to be browsing or couldn't make up their minds between brands. Barry nodded. Regular custom-ers would know what had happened to Gregson and he and Craig had been spotted for what they were. These individuals intended hanging around to find out what was going on. He was about to disappoint them. 'Is Mr Gregson about?'

'He's gone to the bank. He always does about this time on Friday afternoons.'

Barry saw his colleague grit his teeth. And no wonder. Had the woman got no sense? All right, it wouldn't take long for a potential thief to suss this out, but to broadcast it to the world was a different matter. 'Been gone long, has he?'

'Who wants to know?'

Who wants to know. Barry hated the phrase. The obvious answer was 'I do.' Why couldn't people simply ask, 'Why do you want to know?' In reply he held his ID under her nose. 'How long?'

'I don't know. Oh, God, I wish he'd stop.'

For a second Barry thought she was referring to something Tony Gregson did, beat her, maybe, if she was his wife or woman, or gamble away the takings. Only as she went to the door at the back and shouted for the child to shut up did he realise what she meant.

'He's teething.'

The crying infant had reminded him of his own son at home with Lucy. He hadn't thought about him for several hours. Suddenly he wanted to be there. He would never ever shout at his child to shut up. Or so he imagined.

'He won't be long. He knows I can't stay out here for more than half an hour at the moment.'

'We'll wait.'

He and Craig made room for a large female in clothes a size too small. She bustled to the counter and placed a packet of shocking pink coconut mallow biscuits on it, staring at the two men quite openly as she opened her purse to pay. When she had done so she sniffed in a manner which suggested exactly what she thought of the police. 'Bet her old man's done time,' Craig Hanson whispered.

The second customer was paying for her goods when another walked in, followed by a short, squat man whose low forehead and close-set eyes gave the impression he did not like to be crossed. 'Is he still yelling?' He nodded towards the back of the shop. 'Go and see to him, love. I'll take over.' He handed her a yellow cotton cash bag and a paying-in book but she remained behind the counter.

'We'd like a word with you, sir, if we may.' It was Hanson who had spoken because Barry had not immediately recognised the man now that his injuries had healed. He had only seen the photographs where his features had been distorted.

He sighed. 'All right. Upstairs, if you don't mind the noise.'

In the back room of the shop a boy about ten months old was sitting upright in his pram, his face red from crying. He looked miserable and uncomfortable but he was safely strapped in and the room was warm although there was nothing for him to look at apart from cardboard boxes containing goods. Gregson leant down, unfastened his son and removed him from the pram with more gentleness than his observers had expected. He held him against his shoulder and made soothing noises in his ear. The childs body shuddered and he hiccuped an occasional sob but he was soon calmer.

The stairs were uncarpeted but Barry recalled that the shop was a lock-up. The top floor consisted of two rooms, one of which held more stock; the second contained a one-ring burner, a kettle and some ancient kitchen chairs. On a table was all the paraphernalia necessary for a baby.

Gregson took one of the chairs. 'What is it now?' His manner with them was gruff but his grip on the child was still gentle as he turned him on his lap to face the company.

'Look, sir, I know you've already spoken to DC Hanson but this is more serious than we supposed. There've been other attacks of a similar nature. We no longer believe they're random.'

'Well, it's no good asking me any more questions. I've nothing else to say.'

'Have you received any threats recently?'

'Threats? What sort of threat is a man like me likely to receive?'

Barry glanced at Craig. They had both noticed that Gregson had buried his face in his son's neck, possibly to disguise his reaction to the question.

'Threats to your family, maybe?'

'You can damn well leave my family out of this.' As if to demonstrate the point he turned the boy to face him. He began crying again. 'I don't know why I bothered to let you up here. I don't know anything. Now please go and leave us alone. It was bad enough getting beaten up without you lot making it worse.' There was a sheen of sweat on his brow. Gregson ignored it. 'I've got work to do.'

He stood and preceded them down the stairs. Once in the shop he dumped the child in his mother's arms and went behind the counter forcing a smile for a customer waiting to be served. He did not look up as Barry and Craig left.

'Why didn't you ask him outright?' Hanson wanted to know.

'No point. He'd've denied it. Besides, he's scared. They're all scared. And defensive. Not one of them has made a fuss about the lack of arrest.'

'How do we get them to talk?' Craig Hanson scratched his head, knocking Barry in the arm with his elbow as he reached to do so. At the same time his right foot landed in a puddle causing him to curse. 'Not unless something happens to one of their families . . .' Hanson shook his foot and got into the car, banging his head on the roof as he did so.

'We might not necessarily need them to tell us.'

'How come?'

'They're in a no-win situation if it is a protection racket. If they've refused to pay, this is a warning of what's to come if they don't comply or if they go to the police. Or perhaps they've decided they're not going to pay up any more. All three men have people close to them who are vulnerable and – '

'Roberts hasn't got a family.'

'No, but he's still got his own skin to think about.'

'Wait.' Craig suddenly remembered. 'Roberts mentioned that his mother moved here from Wales after his wife left. He wanted her to live at the hotel but she refused. She lives out at Pickerings in one of those bungalows. Sheltered accommodation. But what if they can't afford to pay?'

'You tell me. Without examining their end-of-year accounts we can't tell. However, I reckon they can, that whoever's pulling this scam knows just how far to go. Ask for too much and the business fails and you lose altogether. And I think that the two who are married, their wives don't know, the amounts that have been demanded are reasonable enough so there won't be any questions asked at home.'

'You've got it all worked out, sar . . . Barry.'

'No, you and Campbell had most of it worked out. At least, you were well on the way. Which is all very well, but until we know who's behind it, it means bugger all. Have there been any other – ?'

Barry's question was pre-empted by the answer. 'We put it through the computer. A case some while ago, locals, tried it on but got caught fairly quickly. Jail sentences served and not been seen or heard of in the area since. Several businesses involved. Apart from that, nothing. It's more of a city crime, really.'

'Not any longer, it seems.'

'No, not any longer.'

They returned to the station as the pavements rapidly began to dry and the air was filled with the pungent smell of warm tarmac. To their right a rainbow arched over the hills behind the council estate and in one of the fields the cows, like toys from that distance, were now standing up. They crossed the three sets of lights in Saxborough Road, all in their favour, and headed towards the new part of the town. The Green, where the original hamlet had stood – including the Crown, the Chief's favourite drinking place – was where it had all started, along with the church, of course. Almost four centuries ago both the numbers and the demands of people were fewer: work, food and somewhere to sleep were the essentials, alcohol, religion and the occasional sheep fair the only diversions. St Luke's church had been built not long after the hamlet was formed. Once surrounded by fields and its own small cemetery, it was now incongruous nestled amongst the supermarkets and with the gradual slope of the council estate rising behind it. A wedding was taking place at St Luke's, the bride and groom posing in the lych-gate beloved by the local press photographers and families alike because it provided an easy composition. Several shiny, be-ribboned cars lined the road but the traffic wardens usually turned a blind eye.

They drove down the High Street, past the chain stores where the inhabitants of Rickenham Green could now buy exactly the same goods as everyone else in every other town, and finally entered the area which had once serviced the railway station. The station still existed, a branch line. Barry often wondered if train drivers knew it existed, the service was so poor. The goods depot had disappeared years ago and most of the railway workers' cottages had been de-molished to make way for the new town hall, a concrete and glass edifice, surrounded by other similar buildings from which it would have been indistinguishable except for the coat of arms above the entrance. Linking these architectural nightmares which formed three sides of a square was a pedestrianised area sprouting one or two trees not long past the sapling stage – those that had survived the vandals. On the opposite side of the road was a row of individual shops, all privately owned, the type that Ian claimed to prefer, but the goods they sold defied definition. Apart from the normality of a florist's, a baker's and a dry cleaner's, the goods in the other windows made Barry wonder how the places stayed in business. The inaptly named card shop had a mediocre selection of greetings cards but a plethora of over-priced stuffed toys and cheap gimmicks. The personalised mugs on display in the window bore words so mawkish that they might have served a dual purpose as emetic and receptacle for the consequences. As an insult to the florist another shop sold artificial flowers along with designer gift-boxes which would undoubtedly cost more than the presents put into them. There were plastic sheaves of Suffolk corn and ceramic ashtrays and macramé plant-holders. All this in a town where tourists rarely came unless there were gale force winds on the coast and they fancied an afternoon at the cinema.

'You OK?' DC Hanson was staring at Barry with an incredulous look on his face.

'What?' Barry indicated left to turn into the station car-park.

'You were muttering to yourself. Fatherhood got to you, has it?'

'No, not fatherhood.' But he wondered if that was it. Four or five years ago he would have yawned with boredom if Ian had expressed those same sentiments. Now he was doing it himself. It was, he realised, the first sign of approaching middle age and, despite his intentions, he would probably end up as an old man talking about the good times or, God forbid, beginning sentences with 'In my day'.

They organised their findings or, rather, their instincts into the form of a report then went to discuss them with the Chief.

132

'When DC Campbell returns ask him to come and see me,' Ian instructed when he had learned of the outcome of the interviews. 'See if he's got anything he wants to – what is it they say? – share with us? And I want you to find out if we have any of the big boys paying us a visit. Protection and a shooting don't add up to our villains.'

Ian rubbed the back of his neck and screwed up his eyes against the sun as the earth moved that final degree which meant it shone directly into his office. The pavements were now completely dry. The people down in the street had folded their umbrellas and were carrying their outer garments over their arms. A brief respite from the heat, but no more than that. The late afternoon sky was a vivid blue with no sign of a cloud.

French was being watched, and partly for his own safety. Whoever had set him up, *if* he had been set up, might believe he knew more than he did and had imparted this knowledge to the East Anglian constabulary. They had been talking of the attacks – why had he thought of French? A chain of thought had led him there. Two of the witnesses they had interviewed had not been local. It was a tenuous connection but worth looking into.

On his desk sat the sheet of paper with the hieroglyphics. Later he would study them more carefully. Later. Because he did not want to think what they might mean.

Avril Baker had returned from work on Thursday afternoon relieved to see her husband's car parked outside. With Bill around she would be better able to cope with Joff. They sat outside and chatted quietly, allowing Joff to lead the conversation where he would. As he lay full-length on the grass his strong legs encased in jeans, his bare stomach flat, Avril could not help thinking what a good-looking man he was. His dark hair was full of life and he had a tan although it did not disguise the exhaustion which showed in the lines of his face and the deadness of his eyes. She wondered if he was aware of the impression he created as he lay there chewing a blade of grass and staring at nothing. A little like James Dean, she thought, reaching out to touch Bill's arm.

'I'll give you a hand with the meal,' Bill said as he followed Avril into the kitchen. 'How'd it go earlier?' He inclined his head towards the garden.

'It was difficult. But it's only to be expected. Here, wash these, will you?' She handed him some tomatoes. 'He's still in shock, if you ask me.'

'Bound to be.'

'How long do you suppose he'll stay?'

Bill gathered from this that his wife was not happy with the arrangement, but she would not complain, it was not in her nature. 'I'll ask him myself, in the morning. It hasn't been long after all.'

Avril nodded. Bill was on a late tomorrow. Better he spoke to Joff, man to man. She had put a few items of his clothing in the washing machine along with their own because all Joff had with him was what he had taken on his fishing trip and he refused to go back to the house to pick up a change even though the forensic team had finished there. 'I can't,' he had said emphatically. Avril had offered to go for him but he had shaken his head.

'I think he's holding it all in,' she continued as, between them, they prepared the evening meal. 'I think he feels that because he's who he is, you know, police, he oughtn't to act like other people. He needs a good cry, that's what I think.'

'Maybe.' Bill loosened his collar. 'Not everyone's the same though. I'm going to get out of this lot. I'll be right back.'

Joff came into the kitchen. 'Anything I can do to help? I'll probably be useless, Jassy used to spoil me in that way. She was a good cook.'

She ought to be, she went to some foreign place to learn, and she didn't have much else to do all day, Avril thought, biting her lip immediately, shocked at the uncharitable way her mind was working. She didn't even know the girl. Joff had spoken of her on and off so she had the bare bones of her short life, but it was Avril who had introduced her name each time hoping to help her husband's colleague in some way by doing so. It did not seem to have worked. Joff was as stiff and unrelenting as when he had first arrived.

'No, you go and enjoy the last of the sun while we've got it.'

'That's better.'

Sergeant William Baker had returned clad in an old pair of slacks which were baggy around his buttocks and tight around the middle. The hole of the belt was so worn the leather would soon come apart. Avril sighed. 'That T-shirt doesn't do you any favours.' It was stretched over his ample frame and the round neck made his face seem plumper than it really was. On the front was the name of a lager and its advertising logo. He had won it in a darts competition. Unconsciously Avril was comparing him with the man who had been forced upon them as their guest. As she laid the table she knew which one she would rather share her bed with. Strange, she thought, that it should be Bill.

When they were in bed she whispered, 'Are you sure he's all right? Perhaps he ought to see someone, someone who knows about these things.'

'Time will see to things, love. It always does. I'll have a word in the morning, test the waters, so to speak. He's got relatives, I'm surprised they haven't come to see him.'

Avril turned over. She would be setting off for work at eight thirty. It was a relief to know she could leave things in Bill's steady hands. Joff's grief was so intense it was unbearable to watch. It also made her feel guilty and uncomfortable enjoying such a small pleasure as sitting in the garden.

Joff did not come downstairs until nine thirty by which time Avril had gone to work. He looked worse than on the previous two days and he had not bothered to shave. It surprised Bill to notice a few grey bristles amongst the darker ones. His eyes were puffy so maybe he had cried after all, and his hands shook as he picked up his coffee mug.

'Have you had a chance to make any plans?' Bill asked, deciding to get straight to the point.

'I've been thinking and thinking but I just don't know what to do. I'll have to sell the house, I can't ever go back there. After that, well . . .' He raised a hand in despair.

'Will you stay in the job?'

'Yes, but I'll apply for a transfer, try and start again somewhere else. There's too much here to remind me. And to be honest, Bill, I don't think I could stand the pity.'

'Somewhere near your parents?' Bill's suggestion was not so much out of curiosity as a way of leading on to his more immediate plans.

'No. We don't get on. They did offer me a bed and they're coming to the funeral, whenever that takes place, but we're better off communicating from a distance. They hate the idea of how I earn my living.' He paused. 'I was always a great disappointment to them.'

'Meanwhile? Until you sell the house?'

Joff's head was bent. He shook it. 'I know I can't impose on you any longer, I'll find some cheap digs. Oh, don't worry, I'm not on the breadline, but there's no point in wasting money until the financial side's sorted out. The house'll fetch a good price, assuming what's happened doesn't put people off, and I'll get something smaller. Look, you've been really good about all this, Bill. I'll go out this morning and see if I can find something, perhaps with an evening meal thrown in, if such places still exist. I need to buy a few bits and pieces anyway. You tell Avril that I'll be out of here today or tomorrow.' He leaned across the table and squeezed Bill's arm. 'You've both been great. I don't know what I would've done without you.' He turned away and brushed angrily at his eyes.

Bill nodded. 'You know you're welcome to stay here for as long as you want.'

After that exchange they seemed at a loss for conversation. The kitchen was gloomy. Bill had slept through the thunderstorm but Avril had heard it. Rain ran down the windows in

136

blurred streaks. Nothing beyond it was visible. He decided he ought to offer Joff some breakfast.

'No, thanks. I'm not hungry.'

Yesterday Avril said he had had an appetite. Bill suspected that the reality had only just begun to sink in.

They drank their coffee in silence then Joff went upstairs and came down again carrying the waxed jacket he had taken away with him. 'I'm going into the town centre. Is there anything I can get for you?'

'I don't think so. Avril usually does the shopping on her way home. I'll see you later. Hey, wait, let me give you a key.' Bill rummaged in the drawer next to the sink. It contained things that had no other appropriate place. There were two spares, one of which had been their daughter's.

Joff thanked him and left the house. Bill watched him disappear at the end of the road. Joff's shoulders were hunched but whether from mental anguish or against the rain, Bill could not tell. He made himself some toast and sat down to read the paper, wishing he didn't feel so useless in this situation.

8

'I don't enjoy this.'

'Neither do I,' DC Campbell admitted.

Both forensic experts and scene-of-crime officers had gone through the house in Aspen Close thoroughly. Jasmine Grant's diary and calendar were in the possession of the police and her personal papers had been examined but the Chief had asked them to go back and go through everything one more time. Not as the experts would have done; their role was to find links with the murderer. What DCI Roper wanted was a fresh approach, not clues but incongruity, something that was out of place.

'It's hard,' Brenda continued as she sorted through the dead girl's flimsy underwear. 'It's such an intrusion.'

Alan looked up and blushed. In her hand Brenda was holding a pale blue lace camisole. She swiftly threw it on the bed, recalling the rumours she had heard about his ex-wife. It was before her time at Rickenham Green but it was known that Helen Campbell had performed in pornographic films. Alan hadn't known, not until some videos had been confiscated in a case of suspected child abuse. They had had to watch them at the station in a room equipped for such things and there, in front of several men, including Alan, Helen had appeared on the screen. She was not, she realised, alone as far as rotten marriages went.

They spent an hour in each room. The bedroom yielded nothing more than one would expect to find, except that Jassy's clothes were more expensive than many people could afford. Most of Joff's clothes still hung alongside hers in the wardrobe. His had been given a perfunctory going through on Wednesday, but as he had been away at the time and could prove it, no more had seemed necessary. Besides, Joff had not been back to the house since. If he had had anything to hide he would have returned, hoping to retrieve what might have been incriminating.

Joff's clothes, too, had cost more than the average policeman could afford but Jassy had her own money and was known to be generous with it. 'What else is it for?' one of the Drama Guild had quoted her as saying.

Feeling like a peeping Tom, Brenda reached into the pockets of Joff's jackets. One or two hung in dry cleaner's polythene and all the pockets were empty. Another, smelling faintly of his aftershave, revealed nothing more than a paperclip and a credit card receipt. Brenda could just make out the print. It bore the name of one of the Italian restaurants in the town and the sum, written in Joff's large rounded hand with an addition for the tip, suggested that two people had eaten there. It was dated a week ago. It was a sad reminder of what would never be again if Joff had shared the meal with Jassy.

She felt a sense of relief when neither jackets nor trousers held anything which might be considered sinister. The only thing which was vaguely out of the ordinary was a telephone number written on what appeared to be the torn-off corner of an envelope. Six digits, no dialling code, so presumably a local number, but no name or clue as to whose it might be. Brenda was no expert but even she could see that this was not Joff's writing. There were enough examples of that throughout the house. These figures were thin and sloped to the right. She kept the piece of paper to check against the numbers in Jassy's diary. Although they had made extensive inquiries no trace could be found of either of the Grants indulging in an extra-marital affair, but there was always the possibility that it had occurred, that some girl had given Joff her number.

At the end of the rail were Joff's uniforms. They smelled of the station, the permutations of the smell so familiar yet so difficult to define. These pockets, too, were all empty. Brenda found herself smiling. How different from Andrew, who pulled things from his like a conjurer. Last night had been good. She wanted more nights like that.

Andrew Osborne was tall and fractionally overweight. His nose was hooked and his face scarred by the acne from which he used to suffer. The Chief had called him an ugly brute and, in a way, he was, but there was something about him Brenda found fascinating. It's his gentleness, she decided, pausing briefly from her task. That and his smile. And the way he listens when I speak and even his slightly untidy appearance as if no one had shown him how to dress himself properly. She straightened her back. God, I'm beginning to get soft, she thought, before applying her mind to her job.

'All done, there's nothing here,' Alan said, running a hand through his sandy hair which he had recently had cut so that it stood up on the top of his head about an inch in length, tapering down shorter and shorter at the back and sides. Brenda thought it was a big mistake but did not have the heart to say so.

The bathroom cabinet contained only the usual washing and shaving things. There were no drugs, not even old ones which people tend to store, apart from Jassy's contraceptive pills. The only thing of any medical note was a half-used bottle of TCP. Not wishing to be on the receiving end of the Chief's anger, they even went as far as lifting the lid of the lavatory cistern and tapping the panels on two sides of the bath, but they were solid and fixed.

The other bedrooms were for guests and were beautifully furnished but impersonal. In the upstairs hall was a rectangular card table. On top was an arrangement of dried grasses. Brenda peered into the vase then swivelled the lid of the table. Nothing but green baize. The storage space for cards and score sheets was empty.

'They're not hoarders, are they?' Alan commented surprised at the lack of clutter which most people accumulate in drawers and cupboards, out of sight, even in the best organised of homes.

'Do you suppose a cup of tea would be out of the question?'

'Who's going to know?' Alan grinned. 'Come on, it's thirsty work.'

Brenda put the kettle on but she did not feel comfortable using the dead girl's things. There was milk in the fridge, not in a bottle but in a supermarket waxed container. The date stamp showed it would last several more days. 'We're in luck, I can't stand it black.'

The break was welcome. Murder victims lose their privacy from the moment of their death, as do the people with whom they had been living; in this case Brenda and Alan knew them both, which made what they were doing all the more painful. Joff was one of them and he, more than anyone, would know that what they were doing was essential.

Brenda filled the teapot and folded her arms. 'There, that's my contribution. You can find the cups and things.'

Alan did so, stopping to gaze in astonishment at the exotic ingredients contained in one of the cupboards as Brenda leant against the work surface and watched him.

'Do you think it was Petesy French?' he asked as he carefully took out two bone china cups and saucers.

Brenda shook her head. The shiny hair swung. 'Nope. But that doesn't mean it wasn't.'

'It doesn't make sense to me.'

'It never does. Like life, if you ask me.'

They drank their tea standing up rather than sit at the table in the L-shaped alcove where Joff and Jassy had eaten their last meal together. There were windows on all sides of the kitchen but the day was so dismal they put on the light.

'Come on, let's get finished,' Brenda said when they had drunk the tea and the cups and saucers were rinsed and put away. Leaving everything as they had found it they began on the downstairs.

They were half-way back to the station when the wind-screen wipers packed up. Brenda braked and pulled into the kerb, swearing in a manner which would have shocked Alan's puritanical parents. 'Things like this always happen when you least need them.' She tossed back her hair in exasperation. 'And what're you smirking at, you fool?'

'Your remarkably daft observation DC Gibbons. If it wasn't raining they wouldn't have been turned on and therefore wouldn't have broken.'

'All right, you bloody pedant, get out and fix the damn things.'

She reached beneath the dashboard and released the bonnet catch. Alan pulled up his collar and disappeared around the front, fiddling for a few minutes. 'Try them now,' he called. They still didn't work. 'Ring the station. Put the flashers on. I'll leave the bonnet up.'

Brenda radioed for help whilst Alan made some uninterpretable hand signs before disappearing around the corner, head bent against the rain.

He was hungry again and had remembered that a general store lay only yards down the side road. Opposite it was a paper shop which would carry a wider selection of confectionery. It felt like hours since he had eaten. He darted

141

between cars and crossed the road, his feet slopping in puddles. The shop lights spilled out into the murky street although one of the windows was boarded up.

'Vandalism?' he inquired as he handed over a packet of crisps and a bar of chocolate he had selected from the display.

'Kids, I expect.' The man took his money but did not meet his eyes.

'Your insurers won't like it.'

'They won't . . .' He stopped. 'One pound seven, please.'

Alan handed over the exact amount and walked towards the door. 'Have you reported it?'

'What's it got to do with you?'

'Police,' he said, the one word creating such an air of tension that Alan paused and asked again, 'Have you?'

'No.' The man knew it would be easy to check.

'Why not?'

'God, what's the point? Half the time you lot don't even turn up to take fingerprints and then you never get them anyway.'

'It's still a crime and the insurance companies won't always pay if you don't report it. Besides, how can we ever hope to catch anyone if we don't know it's happened?'

'Look, just leave it. I don't want to make a fuss. I'll pay for it out of my own pocket if necessary.'

Alan hesitated then he came to a decision. He took out his notebook. 'I'm on duty and I'm asking for your name.'

A flash of fear crossed his face as he answered. 'Jack Marshall.'

'All right, Mr Marshall. Thanks very much.'

'Is that it?'

'Yes, that's it. You said you didn't want to make a fuss. Goodbye.'

Alan shut the door behind him. The rain was not as heavy now and he thought it might be clearing up. So, too, might other things if he was correct.

'They'll be about ten to fifteen minutes,' Brenda told Alan as he ripped open the crisps and offered the packet.

142

'Want one?'

'No thanks.'

In no time the empty packet had been stuffed into the map compartment and he was breaking off a bit of chocolate. Brenda said she didn't want any of that either. 'Don't you ever stop eating?'

'Not if I can help it.'

There was a tap on the window. They had not seen the unmarked car pull in behind them. 'Your personal rescue service,' a cheerful voice announced. 'I'll take a quick look. If I can't fix it immediately I'll tow you back.' But some minor repairs were undertaken and the problem was solved.

'Thanks,' Brenda said, giving him one of her best smiles. 'Let's try again.'

Back in the incident room Brenda went through the diary which Jassy had used as an address book and in which was her list of telephone numbers. None of them matched the one she had found in Joff's pocket.

Joff did not notice the rain or feel it seeping through his clothes. He had put on the waxed jacket but left it unzipped. Droplets of water clung to his hair and the fine wool of his sweater across his chest. He couldn't go home, not now, not ever. Impossible to imagine living in that house without Jassy. Head down, hands in pockets, he walked determinedly towards the town centre. Once there he looked in the window of shops which had advertising boards. There was the usual selection of lost pets, cookers for sale and a couple of 'wanted' items. It was almost two hours before he found what he thought he was looking for. He entered the sub-post office and asked the woman serving if she knew whether the advert was still relevant.

'Mrs Jordan's? Yes, as far as I know. She comes in most days and she hasn't said otherwise. And she would've done, I'm sure, because she wouldn't want people knocking on her door day and night for no reason.'

Joff thanked her and turned away. He barely heard her chatter.

'Don't you want directions?'

But he had gone, the door shutting automatically behind him. In the street he headed straight for the address. The woman who answered his knock was in her late fifties but dressed as she must have done two decades ago. Her make-up was overdone and there was lipstick on her top teeth. In contrast her hair was untouched, the greyness unembellished by anything from a bottle.

She showed him the room, taking surreptitious glances at him as she assessed her potential lodger. There was something troubling him, his hands shook and she did not think she had ever seen anyone who looked so exhausted, so utterly defeated. 'Mr Grant?'

'I'm sorry?' She had named the price but Joff had not heard. 'Please forgive me. My wife's just died. I need somewhere to stay for a while. I can't face . . . I can't go home.'

'Oh, you poor dear. You can stay here as long as it suits you. Now come downstairs and I'll make you a cup of tea. And a sandwich if you want. I bet you haven't eaten for a while. Now tell me, when do you want to move in? Today's fine with me, the room's all aired and ready.'

'Thanks. I'm very grateful. You see, I've been staying with friends, they've been really good to me but every time I look at them it brings back memories. I'll get my things and come back in an hour or so.'

'What about that tea?'

'I'm fine, thanks, really I am.' He suspected that the woman would try to mother him but he would keep out of the way. He wanted only to be alone, not to have to make conversation of any sort or think about what life would be like in the future. But like an echo all he heard in his head was the refrain 'Jassy's dead.'

With only a short diversion Joff called at the cash machine outside his bank and withdrew some money because he had little cash on him after paying a week's rent in advance. He

144

put this in his wallet, carefully dividing the notes into their separate denominations, before walking the rest of the way to the Bakers' house. He was relieved to find neither of them in; he did not want to cause offence by saying he had decided to leave so soon. They did not deserve to be hurt and it would be easier for him to leave a note. He wrote a few brief lines, thanking them and saying he would be in touch, and left the small piece of paper propped against the kettle before going to pack his few belongings. When he felt able to face going into a shop he would buy Avril some flowers and a bottle of something for Bill.

Mrs Jordan had gone out of her way to make things comfortable for him and Joff was touched at how kind people could be. There was an extra blanket in the wardrobe, she told him, and a kettle had been placed on a small table near an electrical socket. 'In case you don't want to be disturbed. I don't usually do it,' she added.

Joff did not bother to ask about an evening meal. The house was small and he guessed that he was the only boarder. As pleasant as she seemed to be, it was unthinkable that he could sit down and eat with Mrs Jordan.

There was nothing now to do but wait; for the inquest to be opened, for the funeral or cremation – he had not yet decided which and Jassy hadn't left a will – for the inquest proper and for the police inquiries to be over. And then there was his whole future to consider. One thing was certain, he would have to get away from Rickenham Green.

'It won't be long now, Steph. I've been saving really hard. Just you and me, we'll move away, make a decent life for ourselves. Look, I can't get over until late, about tennish. Is that all right with you or do you want an early night? Good. See you later.' Richard Fry replaced the receiver. The days were slow in passing but it was Friday night, only another week to go. He would spend the weekend with Steph, at her flat which was a better proposition than the room he had.

Fridays were busier than Thursdays and Bilton-Jones would require his services for most of the evening. He'd grin and bear it, it wouldn't be for much longer.

It had rained all day but the evening was fine. Richard wasn't wet, his padded raincoat had served its purpose. When he bought it he had begrudged paying so much money for something simply to keep the rain off but after two weeks in Bilton-Jones's employ he had realised he was expected to be the errand boy and it had proved to be a good investment.

Over forty-eight hours had passed since the body of the policeman's wife had been found and Richard was beginning to relax. Of course he had no proof, nothing at all really except a feeling that Bilton-Jones may know more than he was letting on. He hoped he was wrong and he probably was because he could not think of any reason why the man should want the girl dead. In fact, he realised, Jasmine Grant was more useful alive than dead. It was no longer his problem. He was not and never had been involved and he didn't even know if it was the same gun he had provided which killed her. Soon, very soon, he and Steph would get on a train and make a new start and Steph would be proud of him.

Bilton-Jones opened the heavy wooden front door of his mock Tudor house and strolled out to the waiting car. 'Clearing up,' he said, holding a hand palm uppermost towards the sky, 'Shan't need this.' He threw his Burberry on to the back seat and lowered himself into the front passenger one. 'Usual calls, except a bit quicker tonight. The wife's invited some people around, I said I'd be back by nine.'

Fry nodded as the tyres crunched over the tiny pebbles of the drive. Bilton-Jones spoke little of his wife and Fry had only glimpsed her once or twice, a plain, dumpy figure watching from the doorway as her husband left the house. However, he was astute enough to realise that it was the wife's money which had given him a start in life and that it was her friends who were influential and who could put in a good word as far as the legitimate side of the business was concerned. Bilton-Jones's trouble was that he was greedy, he thought as they made their first call of the evening.

At the same time, Bilton-Jones was thinking how stupid the Ferret was – but that was the reason why he had taken him on. Far better to have someone who did what they were told without asking questions or trying to analyse his motives. He probably didn't even realise that he was involved in anything illegal. Bilton-Jones sighed. His head ached, a hangover from the thunderstorm – they always affected him. He did not know that the pressure he felt was self-induced, that his wife did not care that she had more money than him; in his own mind he felt he had to prove to her and all the people who had known her throughout her life that he was just as good. He may not have been to public school, even if he did allow people to think so, but he had acquired a veneer of confidence and a way of behaving which fooled almost everyone except himself. I'm known on both sides of the fence, he thought. Known and bloody well respected. And I intend to keep it that way.

He was not worried about getting caught, he had covered every angle. If things did go wrong there were others he had set up to take the blame.

'What's up with Campbell? He's like a damn jack-in-the-box.' DCI Roper squeezed his forehead, wondering if there was more thunder to come. In less than an hour the sun had dried everything. Below him he noticed that the soil in the flower beds was already beginning to crumble on top again. The oppressiveness made him lethargic. How nice it would be to go home and sit in the garden, in the shade, and sip a cold beer. But not yet. Things, it seemed, were beginning to move, DC Alan Campbell in particular.

'He's nipped down to see Hanson.' DS Markham spoke with a complete lack of interest. He was busy studying the results of the day's investigations.

'Barry Swan's taken over from him. Can't he accept that?'

No one answered. DC Gibbons and Markham recognised the signs. It was better to remain silent than give the Chief any ammunition when he was in this sort of mood.

A smiling DC Campbell returned.

'Where the hell've you been?'

'Sorry, sir. But I had some information and I thought – '

The smile had disappeared.

'Thank you. Now, can we see what's what?'

Brenda gave Alan a quick smile of sympathy. He had told her in the car what he believed and if the Chief had allowed him to finish what he was saying he would have praised him rather than belittled him.

'Copies of Jassy's bank statements.' Ian threw three sets on to the table. 'Look at them and tell me what you think.'

Three puzzled faces scanned the sheets containing lists of figures. They went back over two years. Each of them took their time, hoping that someone else would speak first because none of them could see any particular inconsistencies. There were no huge amounts withdrawn or paid in, the figures were mostly what one would expect on a statement: a weekly Switch payment ranging from thirty-five to fifty-five pounds to one or other of the supermarkets, cheques for various small amounts and cash point withdrawals, all of which had been made in Rickenham Green. There were also regular monthly payments into the account which were assumed to be the interest from her investments of which Joff had spoken, but this still had to be verified. Other statements from the same bank were addressed to Joff. On these were direct debits for gas and electricity, a few unnoteworthy cheque purchases, a record of his monthly salary paid directly into the account and other, unexplained deposits, none of them large but all around a hundred pounds. Brenda and Alan had reported that Jassy's financial papers had been stored in a drawer but they had found nothing relating to Joff. No building society book, for example.

'I give up.' Brenda pushed the statements away from her and rested her chin on her steepled hands. Air-conditioning or not, she wished someone would open the window. The room was stale and the co-ordinating officer had been sweating.

Ian closed his eyes. Was he mistaken? There was only one way to find out. 'Brenda, I want you to go back and speak to the Goodwins.'

'Again, sir? I don't think there's anything else they can tell us.'

'Again. Take someone with you. Be tactful but find out the financial situation between them and their daughter and Joff. We know they bought the house as a wedding present, but apart from that see if you can discover just how generous they are.'

She nodded, pulling the statements back towards her, and peered at them hard. She got up, glad to be leaving the building but dreading having to intrude upon the Goodwins' grief once more.

Ian's jacket was draped over the back of a chair. In front of him were two used disposable coffee cups stained with the dark liquid. He felt twitchy from a surfeit of it but he still suggested another one. Alan Campbell offered to go and get it. Some vital element was missing from the case but he could not think what it was. Better not to think, much better to allow the information to come in, albeit in dribs and drabs, until they had the complete picture.

'Thanks, Alan.'

He had returned with four plastic containers balanced on a piece of cardboard. The co-ordinator showed his appreciation by means of a wide grin and a thumbs-up signal; Markham accepted his wordlessly.

'OK, Alan, run through this protection thing.'

'We're almost certain that's what it is. This afternoon I came across a man named Jack Marshall. He owns a newsagent's. The window'd been smashed and was boarded up.

Out of curiosity I asked what had happened. He was cagey, said it was kids.'

'What were you doing there?'

Once more the traitorous flush crept up Alan's face. 'Buying crisps, sir.'

Ian raised his eyes to the ceiling. 'Need I have asked?'

'Anyway, he said he hadn't reported it, that he was prepared to pay for the damage himself rather than claim on the insurance.'

'Don't blame him. These things occur so frequently nowadays the cost's often little more than the excess.'

'It's not that. I got the impression he knows who did it. I think it's all connected. Everyone involved in the ABH cases owns a business. There's been no robbery, not even an attempt at one. And no one's talking. We've already ascertained that all the men were attacked as they left work and it looks as if their movements were known to the assailants.'

'Ascertained? Assailants? God, you're sounding more like the CC every day. But yes. And you think that this Marshall bloke's been given a warning, pay up or else?'

'Either that or he's stopped paying and this was a reminder. The thing is, sir, they're all scared and they've all got families to consider. The worrying aspect of it is that these are incidents we know about, there could be dozens of businesses shelling out money.'

'You do realise you're on a murder case, Campbell?'

'Yes, sir.'

'Good. So concentrate on it and let Hanson and Swan do the rest. However, I'm pleased to see you're using your initiative, and well done.'

'Thank you. You see, I had to let them know because of all of them I think Marshall would talk if he was leaned on.'

Ian nodded, feeling ashamed that he was taking his bad mood out on the DC. For two years or more he had hoped the man would gain the confidence to think for himself, now he was doing so his reward was sarcasm from above. An apology was due. Ian swallowed, rubbed his chin and took a sip of coffee. 'I'm tired,' he said, 'and this weather doesn't help. You've done a good job. I mean that.'

'What's missing, here? Can any of you see it?'

'The only thing I can think of is that there's someone else, someone who knew Mrs Grant that we haven't turned up.' Markham finally spoke.

'Could be.' Ian sighed. It seemed only he was thinking in one direction. The obvious one. 'Anyway, with a bit of luck the telephone people will have done their stuff by tomorrow and we'll have a print-out of all their calls. Go on, push off. You can reach me at home if necessary.'

Markham decided to call in at the Black Horse because he had nothing better to do. He never had anything better to do, his home life was non-existent.

9

It was after seven when Ian turned into Belmont Terrace. Not an early end to the week by most people's standards, but reasonable by his. Most of the spaces had been taken but he was able to squeeze his car between two others, cursing the parking of his neighbours. The houses in the terraced street had once been identical but over the years additions had been made as people came and went. There were outside lamps, double glazing, new front doors and a smattering of satellite dishes. The front gardens were small enough to defy the description; a wall, two and a half feet high, separated them from the pavement. Despite their lack of size these gardens illustrated the individuality of the occupants of the houses. Some held a profusion of flowers in pots, one had been made into a miniature rockery with plants which now hung attractively over the wall, another was an ugly concrete patch and one or two were miniature lawns. Ian's was grassed with an evergreen shrub with variegated leaves, the name of which he did not know but which needed no attention. A short path led up to the front door, whose original arched fanlight of stained glass they had decided to retain. Ian's idea of individuality was to change nothing. Let others make the alterations and, without costing him anything, their house would be different.

He got out of the car, locked it and stretched. On both sides of the road windows were flung open; from one of them came the sound of rock music. It blared out into the street and made his head ache further. If that row could be heard inside the house or in the back garden he'd damn well do something about it. Taking the path around the side he passed the kitchen window. Moira was not alone. She and Deirdre sat at the kitchen table with paper and pens in front of them. 'God,' he muttered having been looking forward to a quiet evening. He liked Deirdre very much but anyone's presence apart from his wife's would have been resented.

'Hello. I didn't expect you so soon.' Moira got up and kissed his cheek, just able to do so without standing on her toes. 'Drink?'

'Please.' He saw the wine bottle on the table. Moira and Deirdre hadn't wasted any time.

She poured some beer and handed it to him. 'We're just making a list for the fête. We won't be long. I'll get something to eat then.'

Ian frowned. 'I thought you'd given up all this charity stuff.'

'I have.' Moira grinned at Deirdre. 'More or less. It's just that I've got a donation from the garage and – '

Ian held up both hands in defeat. 'I get it. Don't tell me any more. Where's that bloody music coming from?'

'Oh, that's the Andersons. It's their boys. It isn't that loud. Anyway, it's Friday. They'll be going out soon.'

'And making a din when they come in again, I suppose.'

' Talk about thunder in the air,' Deirdre commented. 'I take it our chief inspector's had a rough day?'

'Your chief inspector has had a worse than awful day. I think I'll take this outside.' He did so, wandering around the large back garden, frowning at the plants and flowers Moria grew so successfully. The effect was pleasing even though he had had nothing to do with it. Suddenly the music stopped and the peacefulness of the evening washed over him. Ian tensed, teeth gritted, waiting for it to start up again. A street door slammed, the sound echoing through the still air, and he heard the voices of youths calling to each other. The Anderson boys are on the loose, God help us all, he thought, sinking on to the bench beneath the tallest tree.

Seeing Deirdre reminded him anew how youthful his wife was. Widowed some years ago, Deirdre had since remained single. She looked older than her age but then, he decided, she always had done – and in fact she had now almost grown into it. She had hardly altered in all the years he had known her.

The beer was cool, its bitterness pleasant on his tongue. Sipping it, Ian began to unwind. How unfair he was to expect Moira to have been alone after all the years he had left her in that state. She was entitled to have anyone she chose in the house. He went inside to make amends.

'I'm just going,' Deirdre informed him with a sideways grin at Moira.

'There's no need. Really.'

'There is,' Moira told him. 'She's got a date.'

'Oh, Moira, you can hardly call it that at my age.' Deirdre looked incongruously coy. Her grey hair was parted down one side and curled under at the ends, her clothes were what Ian thought of as 'county', that is, sensible skirts and shoes and simple blouses or jumpers depending upon the weather. He studied her now, as if seeing her for the first time. He had not noticed that her figure was good, it was fuller than Moira's and she was taller, but everything was reasonably in proportion. And she has a kind face, he decided. Strange that I've never noticed that before.

'Well, being asked out to dinner by a man you hardly

know and who's obviously interested in you is what I'd call a date, wouldn't you, Ian?'

'What? Well, yes, I suppose so.' But Ian was not really listening. The events of the day filled his head, as he knew they would do as soon as he began to relax. He was vaguely aware of the sounds of Deirdre's departure and Moira's voice as he sat at the kitchen table.

Moira saw Deirdre off then said, 'You can move the car if you want.'

'Was that Deirdre's car? The red one? Nice model.'

'She bought it last month. I . . .' She stopped. Yes, she had told Ian but like many things she said it had not sunk in. Now was not the time to point out his deficiencies. Instead she poured another glass of wine. 'I'm working in the morning. Only until twelve, but I expect you'll be going in.'

'Oh, yes. I expect I shall.'

'Ian?' Moira reached across the table. He looked quite grey and she hoped it was only tiredness. 'This one's really getting you down, isn't it?'

He exhaled through his clenched teeth. 'No more than usual, I suppose. And on top of everything else Alan Campbell decides he's got some grey matter and tells me we've got a protection racket going on.'

'Protection?' Moira sipped her drink. The wine was ice cold and very dry. A lightweight plane passed overhead, droning like a large insect, the sound gradually fading into silence. 'I wonder . . . no, it's ridiculous.'

'What is?' Ian looked up. They were alone and it was not yet late. His wife's presence had soothed him, he was beginning to unwind and was ready to listen to whatever Moira was about to say.

'Nothing probably. But living with you all these years has given me an over-active imagination.'

'Out with it, don't keep your old man guessing.'

'Well, it's what Barry said.'

'Barry? When've you spoken to him?'

'Yesterday. I went over to see Lucy and the baby. Remember?'

It seemed longer ago than the previous day and no, he had not remembered. He hadn't seen the boy himself yet. It made him feel guilty.

'He told me about the Taj Mahal. You know, when he left without paying for the meal and they didn't make any fuss about it. I mean, he went back, of course, but he said they just watched him walk out.'

'No! No, don't say that.'

Moira had jumped, shocked at his vehement denial, and spilled her wine on the table. She played with the small puddle, pushing at it with her index finger as she realised the implication of what she had just said.

'Sorry, love. But that's just it, don't you see? That's the one thing I've been trying not to think about.'

'You think the curry house is paying protection money?'

'It's a thriving business, an ideal target.'

'Yes, but they know . . .' Yet another unfinished sentence but Moira knew what was going through Ian's mind. The restaurant staff knew that Barry Swan was a detective sergeant therefore they were either so astonished that he had forgotten to pay that they did not react immediately or – she took a deep breath – or they believed he was not expecting to have to pay. 'Oh, God, not Barry.'

'He told me. It didn't sink in at the time. He made a joke of it. I suppose I didn't want it to sink in.'

'No. Not him. Never.'

'I can't believe it of him.'

'But?' Moira noticed the grim line of his mouth.

'But they have just had a baby and they need to move house and Lucy won't be going back to work for some time.' He paused, shaking his head. 'No, you're right. Besides, he's hardly likely to mention it and he did go back and pay.' So why do I feel so uneasy? he asked himself.

Moira's suggestion seemed to confirm his worst fears but

155

it was best to sleep on it and save any decisions for the morning.

'Nothing ever stays the same,' he commented as they sat down to eat the fish kebabs and rice Moira had dished up.

'Of course it doesn't. Places change, people change. It's natural.'

'Is it? I don't see what's natural about it.'

'I think it's called progress, Ian. Have some salad.' She pushed the bowl towards him.

'You know my views on progress. Now this thing with Barry.' He waved his fork in the air. 'We've worked together all this time, why can't he stay here?'

'I suppose he wants more out of life. Not everyone's happy to stay put.'

'Meaning what?'

'Oh, don't start on me, for goodness sake. I'm not saying I want to move, only that I understand those who do. Anyway, you should be proud of him. You trained him, after all. Can't you see that here he'll always be second fiddle to you? He wants to start with a clean sheet. Change is natural. *I've* changed, almost everyone develops in some way.'

Except me, Ian thought. That's what my wife's getting at. He watched her slender figure as she carried the plates to the sink and realised that he had better change the subject or lay himself open to another accusation of growing more like his father every day.

Markham made his way to the Black Horse, wondering how Brenda was faring at the Goodwins'. DC Hanson would be following up Alan Campbell's lead and Barry Swan was doubtless at home mooning over his infant son. The Chief? Markham's mouth twitched. At home too, nursing a beer if he's got any sense, he thought.

The pub door was wedged open with a piece of wood but the usual combination of chips and smoke and spilled beer wafted out to meet him. It was as busy as he had expected for a Friday night. The juke-box prevented the possibility of conversation, but it was not a place where people came to converse. They came to mix with their own kind and to drink or, if they were lucky, to pick up a girl or a woman. There were already several clutches of females, drinks in their hands, eyeing the men, but being ignored because it was too early in the evening for pairing off.

Markham used to despise the men who so casually chatted up the girls before taking them home, or wherever it was they went, for sex but he soon came to realise that the females were just as predatory as the men, if not more so. Two of them were watching him now, their intentions obvious. He gave them a curt nod, which was more insulting than ignoring them, and continued to the bar.

In the right-hand corner was the usual crew, including Petesy French and Mark Howard, both of whom furtively averted their faces. French was not the type to disappear – anything other than his own territory was beyond his comprehension. Even if he proved to be guilty his habits were too fixed to allow him to make a run for it.

Over the deafening noise Markham shouted his order and placed some money on the bar. He saw Richard Fry speaking to Bilton-Jones at the far end of the counter and took it all in. Fry had an orange juice in front of him which he drank in two gulps. There was nothing unusual in that. Fry did all the driving. Two minutes later the pair had left. His attention was distracted by Mark Howard who, catching Markham's eye, flinched and bent down, ostensibly to tie up the lace of his trainers. Markham nodded again. Mark Howard had something to hide. He swallowed the rest of his drink and turned slowly. 'OK, Howard, outside,' he said.

'What? Me? I haven't done anything.'

'Who says you have?' Markham pushed his way through the increasing crowd without waiting to see if the boy was following him. He knew that he would be, that someone like Mark Howard was easily intimidated. Outside Markham blinked against the evening sunshine which was blinding after the dimness of the bar. He turned to face the door and saw the fear in Howard's face as he came to meet him.

'Let's take a walk. Just around the corner.'

The terror increased and Markham knew it. Inwardly he was smiling. His presence alone created fear but he knew that the boy had misinterpreted his words and thought he was in for a spot of police brutality. Nothing was further from Markham's mind but it would not do any harm to allow the boy to believe it for a few seconds longer.

They turned into a residential road. Markham stopped walking and faced Howard. 'What's going on?'

'What do you mean?'

'I mean with you and Fry.'

'Nothing.'

'Nothing. Fine, then you can come down to the station with me and tell the others that. I saw the way you were watching him. What's he said to you? Tell me now and you can get back to your scumbag mates.'

'Look, I don't know. He came up to me the other day and asked if I'd be interested in taking over from him.' Mark Howard was short and thin but with a healthy complexion and good teeth. His eyes were a greyish green and golden flecks danced in the irises. His nose had been broken at some point, a fact which had done him a favour by preventing him from being too pretty. He ran a hand through his spiky hair and his mouth trembled. 'Jesus. He swore me to secrecy. If this gets out, that I've told you, well . . .'

'Well what?'

'I don't know.'

'Has someone threatened you?'

'No.' He seemed to relax.

'Then listen to me, you little creep, I'm threatening you. I want to know everything and I want to know it now. There's something going on in that pub, something which may be connected to the murder of an officer's wife, and I want to know what it is.'

Mark Howard licked his lips. 'All right. The Ferret wants

out, he told me so. He knows I can't get work and he thought I'd be grateful.'

'Richard Fry wants out? I'd have thought he's on to a cushy number.'

'Oh, he is, but he's got this girlfriend, see, and he wants to go off and live with her.'

'Why can't he move in with her here?'

Howard shrugged, looking as nonplussed as he felt. 'Perhaps he doesn't like it here.'

'Don't mess me around, son.' Markham took a step closer and, as if it had been choreographed, Howard took one backwards.

'I'm not. Honest. I don't know any more than that. Fry wants out and he offered me the job.'

'*He* offered you the job. I thought he worked for Bilton-Jones. And if Fry's leaving is a big secret how do you know Bilton-Jones would want you?'

'It's more complicated than that. Bilton-Jones does want me to go and work for him, it's just that he doesn't know Richard wants out.'

Markham shook his head. 'You've got a driving licence?'

'Yes.'

'Legal?'

Howard looked hurt. 'Of course it is. Passed my test seven years ago and never had any driving convictions. I just can't afford a car, that's all.'

'So tell me, sunshine, why aren't you keen on the offer? You don't want to work, is that it, when you can ponce off the state?'

'No. I just . . . well, I just don't fancy it.'

'Either there's something you're not telling me or you're work-shy. I think we'd better take a longer walk, down as far as the station. And there's no choice about it this time.'

For a split second Markham's adrenalin flowed as he waited to give chase but if the idea of making a run for it had crossed Howard's mind he had thought better of it. 'What about my drink?'

'Bugger your drink. You'll have to make do with canteen coffee.'

Together they walked down the High Street and on towards the station. Markham, who travelled everywhere possible on foot, did not bother to call a patrol car to collect them and Mark Howard was too frightened to protest. The unlikely pair walked up the steps of the police station together as if they were old friends.

DC Craig Hanson had been told by Alan Campbell that Marshall's paper shop stayed open until nine. He glanced at his watch with its round plain face and leather strap. It had belonged to his father and he was proud to wear it. It also kept good time. Seven twenty. He yanked his jacket off the back of his chair. It had been necessary earlier in the day but now the humidity was building up again and he was grateful that his shirt was short-sleeved. In the downstairs Gents he checked his hair in the mirror, sighing at the one or two strands of grey which marred the overall blackness. Another legacy from his father who had had thick strong hair once, as dark as his own, but which had greyed early.

He had missed the bulk of the traffic so it did not take long to reach the shop. Lights were on and the window was still boarded up. Hanson parked on the single yellow line, locked the car door and went inside. Customers were studying the magazines and journals on display in the racks. One woman was actually reading one of them. Beneath were newspapers: the national dailies and a stack of *Rickenham Heralds* which came out on Friday morning but which many people did not bother to buy until the weekend proper. Craig Hanson cringed when he saw the photograph of Jasmine Grant on the front page. What on earth would it do to Joff? He approached the till. Customers would be coming and going until Marshall closed because he also sold cigarettes and confectionery and one or two basic items such as bread and milk which was kept in a tall glass-fronted refrigerator along with soft drinks

160

and fresh orange juice. His wife believed he was working late. He had no intention of waiting until nine, not with PC Tricia Harding awaiting his attention. Discreetly he produced his identity. No point in making a big show of things and being accused of harassment. 'Can we have a word?'

Jack Marshall's eyes flicked rapidly around the shop. 'Can't you see I'm busy?'

'Isn't there someone else who can take over for a few minutes?'

'No, there isn't. There's only me at this time of day.'

Hanson sighed. There was no way in which he could force the man to close early. All they had was DC Campbell's suspicions to work on and what Marshall had told him might well be the truth. He nodded, knowing there was nothing for it but to return later.

There was no evidence, only an unreported broken window. 'I'll be back at nine. Make sure you're here or I'll have to catch you at home.'

Marshall nodded and tried to be polite to the woman who placed a *Herald* on the counter. 'Dreadful, isn't it? No one's safe these days,' Craig heard her say as he left the shop.

Swearing under his breath, he went to find a phone box where he dialled the number Tricia Harding had given him. An unknown female voice answered. 'Oh, hi. I'm Gloria, one of Tricia's flatmates. She said you might ring. The thing is, she's not here. She's had to go out.'

'Out?' Craig Hanson looked at his watch again. He wasn't due to meet her until eight thirty. 'How long will she be?'

'She didn't actually say, only that she'd be late and that if you rang I was to apologise for her.'

'I see.' And he did. He'd been stood up, made a fool of and would no doubt be laughed about in the female locker room.

'Any message?'

'Only that I was ringing to say I couldn't make it either.' He wished he hadn't bothered, it had sounded like sour grapes but it was too late to worry about that. He hooked his thumb into the tag at the neck of his jacket, flung it back over one shoulder and stomped down the road to the park. It wasn't much of a park. There was an area with a slide and three swings, beneath which the council had recently fixed rubber matting to prevent children breaking their necks on the concrete into which the things were riveted. The rest was scruffy grass, now yellowed and, in places, so bare there was only the dry earth. The shrubs which lined the railings looked tired and dusty and, despite the signs erected in one roped-off corner which was for the use of dogs, Hanson noticed there was dog shit elsewhere, shrivelled up in the sun.

He found a bench and sat down, slouching against its hard back. Some children shrieked in mock fear at a game in which they were involved amongst the bushes, their leaves and branches shaken as if they were being ravaged by a storm. A law-abiding elderly lady walked a small dog on its lead over to the designated area. The seats formed a semicircle on one side of the park. Craig Hanson stared at the face of the occupant of another seat. A young man – in his mid-twenties, he guessed – sat, legs apart, forearms on his knees, his head bent in the typical pose of defeat or despair. He was smartly dressed and did not have the appearance of an addict or alcoholic unable to get a fix. More than likely he, too, had been stood up. Perhaps he had arranged to meet his woman on that very park bench. I know just how you feel, mate, Craig sympathised, although he wasn't exactly heart-broken as he hardly knew Tricia and had never taken her out before. His pride was hurt, no more than that, and he did have a wife.

Other people strolled past, some dressed up for an evening out. Two girls in skirts so short they were hardly worth wearing tossed their long hair over their shoulders as they passed him. They gazed at him openly and giggled as they went on. One of them had said something which he was unable to hear. 'I hope your mothers know you're out,' he called after them spitefully, feeling the whole of the female sex was against him.

Moodily he stood up and left the park by the bottom

162

entrance which led into a lane to the High Street. A circular walk would take him back to the shop where he would conduct the interview with Marshall. Out of the corner of his eye he caught the gleam of reddish brown hair as a car indicated to turn left at the traffic lights. It was DC Brenda Gibbons returning from whatever assignment she had been on. The Grant case, of course. With an empty Friday night ahead of him, Hanson determined to crack his own case long before the murder was solved even if he had to drag it out of Marshall. But it was easier than he could have hoped.

Jack Marshall was pulling down the shutters when DC Hanson returned. Three loaves of sliced bread stood on the counter, waiting to go on top of the pile when tomorrow's delivery arrived. 'I thought you weren't coming back. Come on out here. If people see me in the shop they'll be banging on the window for something.'

Hanson followed him down the length of the shop, glancing up at the magazines on the top of the racks. There were the usual titles, nothing out of the way and placed where they should be in accordance with the law. Marshall had gone one better. The magazines overlapped so that only the first few letters of the name of the publication could be seen, which was enough for regular readers.

A door led into a combined store room and kitchenette. Along one side of the wall were stacked cardboard cartons of soft drinks and boxes containing sweets and chocolates. Another small door, in the wall itself and made of steel, was shut and locked. Marshall saw Hanson's glance. 'The safe. I keep the cigarettes and tobacco in there.'

'Good idea.'

'I don't carry a huge stock, there's no point when they deliver regularly.'

But they were not there to discuss his business habits, sensible though they seemed to be.

Marshall pulled out one of the two chairs from beneath a table covered in a plastic checked cloth. 'It's been a long week and I want to go home. What can I do for you?' Marshall was

163

shorter than Hanson and on the thin side. He had a small moustache which drooped beneath a slightly bulbous nose, giving him a sad expression. Although he was clean and his clothes were well cared for, he had a somewhat seedy appearance as if he'd spent too long without fresh air.

'About your shop window – '

'Oh, God, not that again. Haven't you got better things to do with your time? There's been a murder and you're bothering me about a poxy smashed window.'

'There's more to it than that, isn't there, Mr Marshall?' DC Hanson had also sat down. He leant back and crossed his legs, making himself comfortable, as if he was prepared to stay for a long cosy chat. Why not? He had nowhere else to go now.

'What do you mean?' Jack Marshall's voice was gruff and he snapped the words out more quickly than he had intended.

'I think you know who did it.'

'If I did, I'd get them to pay for it.' Colour flooded his face and DC Hanson knew he had him.

'Wouldn't you pay?'

'What?'

'You heard me. You decided not to pay so you were given a warning. You read the papers, you know what's happened to three other businessmen in this town.'

Marshall looked down at his knees. Yes, he had read of the three cases and he had wondered. If what this man was saying was true, then he could be the next in line. So far he had only been approached but he had said he couldn't afford to pay the sum being asked. It wasn't true, the sum was not extortionate, but he did not see why he should leave himself and his wife short. Nothing had been said, other than if the conversation was ever repeated Marshall should start thinking about retirement because cripples can't work. The man who came had then quietly left the shop. The following night the window had been smashed. He knew this was his opportunity, to tell DC Hanson what he knew and to give a

164

description of the man, whose name he did not know. Perhaps they could stamp it out, make it safer for everyone. It was strange, only an hour or so previously he had decided he had no option but to pay. He could not afford to get beaten up and he could not afford to cause his wife, Jeannie, any worry. She was what her mother called highly strung, but Jack Marshall knew it was more than that. She was neurotic and needed medication to keep her on an even keel. Something like this would cause a relapse and maybe another spell in the psychiatric wing of Rickenham General. He swallowed nervously as he came to a decision. If he kept quiet it was possible that someone else might talk which would leave him in the clear. He had no idea how much the police knew so maybe he need not be involved at all. But the man opposite him was giving nothing away. He sniffed, took a deep breath and began to talk.

When Detective Constable Craig Hanson left the shop he was accompanied by Jack Marshall who had rung his wife to say he would be late home. He had given her a plausible enough excuse about stock lists. Marshall had agreed to make a statement in return for which Hanson had said that someone would keep an eye on his house until he got home. All thoughts of Tricia Harding had faded from his mind.

It had taken Brenda Gibbons ten minutes to find a free detective to accompany her to the Goodwins' house. It was a man she did not particularly like because he was of the opinion that any female within his reach was game. He was, she thought, out of the same mould as Harry but she refused to let him rile her because she was convinced that in the not too distant future she would be promoted over his head and that would be a beautiful recompense.

They had driven to the house in silence once DC Pearson realised there was no mileage in winding DC Gibbons up.

It had been a brief interview but long enough for Brenda to ask the right questions, ones which gained her the begrudging admiration of DC Pearson; however, although they had the answers, neither was sure what they meant.

'Would you mind dropping me in Deben Lane?' DC Pearson asked politely with no sign of his earlier lasciviousness. 'Only there's a witness I've got to see. Might as well do it now.'

Pearson got out of the car and gave her a wave as he set off towards one of the big houses set back from the road. Brenda made a three point turn and went back up Deben Lane, turning left at the traffic lights which took her into the High Street.

At the main entrance of the station she almost collided with Markham who was ushering a frightened-looking specimen towards the interview rooms. As taciturn as usual, he merely nodded and went on walking. She would find out what he was up to before she contacted the Chief at home. He might not appreciate being disturbed on a Friday evening but better incur his wrath now than later if he had not been informed.

She leant against the corridor wall, grateful for its coolness through the thinness of her dress. No, no, no, she silently repeated. Yet what other explanation could there be? Markham, having settled his man, poked his head around an interview room door. 'Want to sit in, or are you off home?'

To what? Brenda thought. 'What's he done?'

Markham explained as she listened, head tilted to one side. 'Yes, but you'd better listen to this first. And I think we ought to ring the Chief before we carry on.'

Markham shook his head, his lips a grim line. 'It happens,' he said phlegmatically. 'Shame it had to happen here. If you're right, that is. You ring him, I'll see that Howard gets some tea. I think he needs it.'

Brenda raised her eyebrows knowingly. So would anyone who had spent ten minutes alone with Markham. She got an outside line and dialled Ian's home number. It was Moira who answered. 'Yes, he's here. Hold on.' In the background she could hear the faint sounds of a television set and a murmur of voices.

166

'Roper here.'

'Sorry to disturb you, sir, but I thought you'd want to know.' She paused to draw breath. 'It seems it might be worse than we thought.'

Ian listened, feeling the muscles in his stomach tighten in apprehension before a wave of nausea washed over him. He was aware of Moira, standing silently beside him, aware that she had guessed what was happening.

'He's coming in,' Brenda told Markham who had returned. 'He wants to interview the Howard kid himself.'

They stared at each other, for once on the same wavelength. One of their own was on the make, possibly more than one. It reflected badly upon them all.

'It's for you. Here, give him to me.' Lucy reached for baby Martin and held him confidently. The telephone had not woken him.

Barry frowned. 'Who is it?'

'Ian.' She nuzzled the child's soft head and sat in a chair watching his sleeping face.

'Hi. When're you going to see your namesake? Well, almost your namesake.' Barry smoothed back his hair and turned to face the window which looked out at the back of the large first-floor lounge. Two men were just locking up the body-shop and on the other side of the wall which divided two business premises he saw a couple of workers from the meat pie depot standing in the yard for a cigarette break. He quite liked the industrial flavour of their rear view, but now somewhere larger was required, preferably a house with a garden.

'What?' Suddenly he understood the tone of voice. He was being questioned.

'I said will you tell me again about that curry you didn't pay for?'

'There's nothing to tell. I was so busy thinking about Martin I forgot to pay. And I did pay. As soon as I remembered I went back. What the hell are you getting at, Ian?'

167

'I have to ask.'

'You have to ask? Jesus. You think . . .' For several seconds he was unable to speak. 'I don't believe you, I really don't. And let me remind you of a man higher up the ladder than you who left under a cloud. Are you above suspicion?' Anger made him say it. Barry knew more than anyone that the answer was yes.

'Barry?' Lucy went to his side and touched his arm with her free hand. He shook it off.

'Look, I'm going in, if you – '

But Barry did not hear the rest. He had slammed down the receiver uttering a string of oaths. He'd got his promotion, he'd got his family to think of. Any hint of Ian's suspicions and he'd be the loser. Mud sticks. Seeing his wife's stricken face and hearing his waking son's yells he controlled his temper. 'Will you be all right on your own for a while?'

'Of course I will. And I'm not alone.' She watched from the window until the tail lights of Barry's car disappeared then she put Martin in his pram, wheeled it into the kitchen and shut the door on his cries before dialling Moira's number.

They met in the general office: Markham, Brenda, Ian and Barry. Coffee had been provided and they each took a seat. 'You start,' Ian said to Brenda. He and Barry had not exchanged a word.

'The Goodwins knew nothing of Joff's financial position. They have never given him any money. Each of the daughters was set up with a property of their own, Jassy owned the one in Aspen Close, but that was the extent of it. The Goodwins initially suspected Joff had married their daughter for money but they wanted their children to make their own way in the world once they had provided them with somewhere to live. There were no investments, they assumed Joff had a private income.

'Mr Goodwin admitted that they weren't as flush as many might think and that he and his wife intended enjoying their retirement to the full. They were not in a position to give money away. However, they said at least they knew both their girls had a roof over their heads.'

At least he and Moira wouldn't have that problem, there wouldn't be a great deal to leave. For once he was glad that Mark was so very independent, they would not need to worry about him coping. 'Jassy didn't discuss her finances with them?'

'No.'

As the news sank in, a silence filled the room, more oppressive than the weather. It was Ian who broke it. 'We know what Joff's salary is – do we know if he had any other source of income?'

No one wanted to answer. Ian nodded. 'I thought not.' He sighed deeply. 'OK, you know what needs to be done.'

They were all wondering whether this had any relevance to Jasmine Grant's death.

'Come on, let's see what this Howard lad's got to say for himself. You coming, Barry?'

DS Barry Swan had not spoken since he entered the room. His fury was abating but he still could not believe that Ian had thought him capable of being involved in whatever Joff had been up to. He followed him downstairs where they found Mark Howard nervously picking at his empty plastic cup. His eyes widened in fear when he saw the two men and they introduced themselves by rank. 'I haven't done anything,' he said immediately.

'We just want to ask you some questions. You're not under arrest.' It was obvious by the surprise on Howard's face that he had believed that he was. Typical Markham, he'd terrified him.

Mark nodded but didn't look reassured.

'You're a friend of Peter French, I understand?'

'Yes.'

'So you know that he was under arrest?'

'Yes. But he didn't do anything. He never killed that girl. Not Peter.'

'He told you this?'

'He didn't need to. Anyone could tell he didn't do it.'

'Did he mention anything about her or about the gun?'

'No. And if he'd had a gun, I'd be the first one to know.'

'Why's that?'

'Petesy's not exactly shy. Something like that, well, he'd have boasted about it.'

'All right. Let's move on to Richard Fry. How well do you know him?'

'I don't. Not really. He comes in the pub with that Bilton-Jones bloke, that's all I know.'

'Except he offered you a job. At least, that's what you told Sergeant Markham.'

Howard nodded enthusiastically, anxious to get it all off his chest. He really hadn't done anything wrong and it seemed that they knew nothing about the video cassettes. 'He's seen me in the Black Horse, of course, but he just came up to me one day, last week, it was, and says, well, he says he's thinking of moving away, setting up with his girlfriend, but that I wasn't to breathe a word of it. He asked if I'd like his job.'

'And what, exactly, is his job?'

'He drives Bilton-Jones around.'

'And that's it?' Ian watched his expression carefully. It seemed that Mark Howard really knew very little but Ian was sure he suspected something.

'He has to pick things up sometimes. He said there's regular calls but that the work's dead easy and he'd put in a word for me. I think he's a bit afraid of letting Bilton-Jones down and he wanted to have someone lined up ready for when he left.'

'But Bilton-Jones isn't aware he's about to lose his employee.' It was a statement. 'I wonder why Fry wanted to keep it a secret?'

Mark Howard shrugged. 'I dunno.'

'So tell me,' Ian continued conversationally, 'what is it you think Fry has to collect?'

170

'I don't know.' But the answer came too swiftly. 'I said I didn't want the job.'

'Why not? You're unemployed and no doubt he pays well.'

'I just didn't want it. I couldn't take being ordered around by someone like that.'

'It couldn't be that you knew it was out of your league?'

'What's that supposed to mean?' He looked offended.

'That this was something bigger than you're used to, something a lot more serious than fencing the odd bits of stolen property?'

Howard didn't answer.

'Tell us. For your own sake you must tell us.' It was Barry who spoke. And for mine, he had added silently.

Mark Howard, a coward at heart, misinterpreted this comment too, assuming it was the detectives who posed a threat. 'Look, I don't know anything, not for certain. And if it's true, and they find out I've talked, whatever happens to me'll be your fault.'

'Nothing's going to happen if you tell the truth.' Ian hated himself for saying it. It often wasn't the case.

Howard looked from Ian to Barry, who nodded his encouragement. 'All right, I can't swear to it but I think they pick up money. I've looked in his car, Bilton-Jones's car, there's never anything in it, unless whatever it is they pick up is in the boot. And once I thought I saw Tony hand over some money. I couldn't swear to it, though.'

They let the first part go. No doubt Howard had his own reasons for staring into people's vehicles. Theft from automobiles was just in his line. 'Tony?'

'Yeah. Tony Peak, the landlord at the Black Horse.'

'Let's get this straight,' Ian continued. 'You thought that you saw Tony Peak handing money over to Richard Fry?'

'No. To Bilton-Jones. But like I said, I couldn't swear to it.'

'So that's why you refused the offer of the job, you knew it was way over your head.'

'If you say so.' He sat back, arms folded, almost proud of himself.

What neither Ian nor Barry could understand was how someone like Mark Howard had been able to spot it. Richard Fry must surely have said something more. Markham had had his suspicions that something was going on there but he hadn't spotted it and Markham was no fool. Of course, the clientele knew who the sergeant was. They would pick their moments carefully. Hearsay though it was, they had enough to bring them in. About to issue instructions, Ian was interrupted by a knock at the door.

'Sir, I thought you should know ...' A constable walked across to Ian and spoke quietly so only he could hear. 'DC Hanson's just brought in a Jack Marshall. He says he's had his shop window smashed because he refused to pay protection money.'

Ian's frown disappeared to be replaced by a slow smile. For a second he thought he had been interrupted to be informed of some small act of vandalism. 'Does he now? Then we'd better have a word with him.'

'He also says his wife's been undergoing psychiatric treatment and she can't be left alone for too long. Shall I send someone over?'

'Get a WPC to go over and have a word. I suppose she can sit with her for a while but only if she can't find a neighbour or relative to come in. We're not a private nursing agency.'

'Can I go?'

'What?' Ian had almost forgotten the presence of Mark Howard. 'Yes. But we may need to speak to you again.'

'I shan't be leaving the country, if that's what you mean.'

'And keep away from the Black Horse for the next few days.'

He did not need telling. He wouldn't be seen anywhere in the vicinity of the place.

After Mark Howard had been sent home in a police car Ian sat in on DC Hanson's interview with Jack Marshall. The same police vehicle had been used to despatch a WPC to the home of Marshall's wife with strict instructions to play down her husband's whereabouts and his involvement.

Time was catching up on him. Ian had been awake since a little after six having been disturbed by the thunderstorm. He was not up to conducting a second interview straight after the first and it was better to let Hanson have his turn. He needed the experience.

Jack Marshall stated his name and address then described how a man had come into his shop, bought a packet of cigars, lingered until another customer had been served then said his piece. 'Fifty pounds a week, that's what he wanted. No more than that, he said, as if it was nothing.'

'Did he threaten you in any way?' Hanson asked, although he already knew the answer. This was for the record.

'Not exactly.'

'Will you explain, please?'

'He said he was sure I didn't want any problems, that there was a lot of crime on the streets these days, then he said that he knew where I lived. That was the first time.'

'Did he ask you for any money on the spot?'

'No. He said he had a friend who would be calling on me. I said I didn't care if it was the Archbishop of Canterbury, I didn't see any reason why I should part with my hard-earned money. I work damn long hours in that shop. The next day another man came and asked if I wanted to be a cripple. That night my window was broken. I had decided I could afford fifty pounds after all.' Marshall's tone was ironic. 'I've been expecting someone to call in at any time.'

It was likely that the presence of first DC Campbell then DC Hanson had been noticed. In which case, Ian thought, Marshall or his wife could be in serious danger. It was as well a WPC had been sent to sit with her.

Marshall was then asked for a description of the men in question and provided them with details which proved him to be a very observant witness.

To be on the safe side Marshall was shown out via the back door. He was adamant that he wanted to make his own way home, he did not want to be seen getting out of a police car, then he realised that it might be too late, that there was already a policewoman in the house. He had placed his wife in danger. But he had also done his duty and he felt better for it. If he took a beating, so be it, as long as his wife wasn't harmed.

Ian and Craig left the interview room, taking the sealed tape with them to be stored. 'I want everyone in the incident room now.'

Barry was already there, kicking his heels until he heard the final outcome of the interview. He was no longer angry but he wanted a word in private with Ian.

'This has to be synchronised. I want everyone brought in at the same time. Or, at least, I want them all to be able to see each other. Fry, Bilton-Jones and the three men who were attacked.' He ticked them off on his fingers.

'And Joff?' It was Brenda who asked the question they all wanted the answer to. So far they had been unable to trace his whereabouts. William Baker had said he had left a note explaining that he needed to be alone to think. Men were out there now trying to find him.

Together they worked out the details. The description Marshall had provided fitted Bilton-Jones. This, in turn, tied in with what Mark Howard had told them. 'With a bit of luck they'll all be tucked up in their beds and we won't have to look far,' Ian added as they filed out of the room.

The surveillance on Petesy French continued. Knowingly or unwittingly he had been involved in a murder. The gun was found in his possession. As the net tightened his chances of survival decreased.

It was half-past one in the morning and the reception area was busier than at some points during the day. With more precision than Ian had expected, the people involved had been roused from their beds, given five minutes to get dressed and brought in. With the exception of Joff who seemed to have disappeared.

Bill Baker had opened the door with a dishevelled-looking Avril standing close behind him. 'He hasn't come back,' Bill

174

had said with astonishment when he learned of the reason for their persistence in wanting to know Joff's whereabouts. 'And he's taken all his stuff with him, not that it amounted to much.'

Bill was more than grateful to be on a late the following day. He put his arm around Avril and they went back to bed.

Back at the station Ian was tapping his teeth with a pen. Where did they start to look for Joff? If he wasn't in a bed and breakfast or boarding house he could be in a room in any of the private houses in Rickenham Green. If he hadn't already left the area. No point in advertising for him, he thought, if he's involved he'll just make a run for it.

Ian was too tired to be of any use. He left the interviewing of Bilton-Jones *et al* to other detectives but there was one more thing to check before he went home.

Ian was amazed at how many trains travelled to Edinburgh and back from London, leaving from Euston, King's Cross or Waterloo for the sleepers. Joff Grant had travelled from King's Cross, the easiest to reach.

With timetables and his sheet of hieroglyphics in front of him, Chief Inspector Roper came to a decision.

'S. 0745 I. 0853 LS. 1000 KC. (FS) 1412 E.' Straightforward and checked out. On Saturday Joff had caught a train from Ipswich at a quarter to eight and arrived at Liverpool Street a few minutes before nine giving himself ample time for the tube ride to King's Cross where he had boarded the ten o'clock Flying Scotsman to Edinburgh. He was met at Waverley station at two fifteen.

The return journey, though, was a different matter. Joff had certainly arrived in Ipswich on the train on which he told Jassy to expect him. But, Ian thought, and it was a big but . . .

Joff had not been seen at breakfast.

'W. 0600 0610 (7 8 9) then ½ hourly. JT approx 4½ hrs. LS to I hourly except rush hours when ½ hrly. JT 1hr 5m – 1hr 13m.'

Two trains departed from Waverley around 6 a.m., one on the hour for the next three hours then as frequently as half-hourly. The trip took roughly four and a half hours. Allow time to get to Liverpool Street then there was an hourly service to Ipswich, half-hourly during the rush hours.

If Joff had caught an earlier train than the ten thirty on which he was booked he could have been in Rickenham Green by – when? – twelve, twelve fifteen, have killed his wife, returned to Liverpool Street on the 1345 or even the train an hour later and, exhausting as it seemed, come back to Ipswich on the four o'clock which arrived at thirteen minutes past five when he was due to be met by his wife.

Three times Ian looked at the timetables and compared them with his calculations. Not only possible, he concluded, but possible with several variations. He left word that he wanted Jeremy Prangnell contacted first thing in the morning. Trying not to yawn ostentatiously in front of the night shift he went downstairs and out to his car, glancing up at the sky as he did so. There was some cloud against the backdrop of blackness and the slightest of breezes rustled the leaves on the trees. He would not be sorry to see the end of this summer.

On Saturday morning he left the house an hour before Moira, promising to be home around lunchtime or just a little later. By then it would all be over.

As soon as Jeremy Prangnell, the organiser of the fishing trips, had told them what they wanted to know, the search for Joff Grant intensified.

Prangnell was an early riser and was always up to supervise the breakfasts for the guests. He had already confirmed that Joff Grant had not been present at breakfast on the last day of his stay and it was believed he had left before it was served.

A second telephone call elicited the names of the only two taxi drivers in the area but they were not immediately available, both being out on jobs. Joff Grant had said he had taken a taxi that morning as individual arrangements had to be made for the return journey. If indeed he had, then he could be in the clear, If not, then they were back to square one and there was no way of proving what his movements had been once he had left the fishing resort.

Mrs Jordan's name was not on their list of rental accommodation but it did not take long to find her. Word of mouth, especially in corner shops, more especially in ones which opened early to receive the daily papers, was a powerful tool. Mrs Jordan's card was no longer in the widow of the post office-cum-stores but the lady serving recalled Joff coming into the shop because he had seemed in such a hurry. Mrs Jordan was contacted and told that under no circumstances was she to alert her temporary boarder that they wanted to speak to him and that someone would be there in a very short time.

'He's still asleep,' she had said, pulling her dressing-gown tightly around her as if it could protect her from whatever nastiness was about to take place under her roof.

Joff had heard the telephone ring. It was an old-fashioned one with a bell. However, as nobody knew where he was he was not concerned. He got up to use the bathroom as by that time Mrs Jordan was in the kitchen. He would not sleep now so he decided he might as well get dressed and go down and see if there was a cup of tea available. He did not yet know the routine of the house.

'I hope the phone didn't wake you.' Mrs Jordan straightened her hair and managed a smile. 'It was my son, he's such an early riser.' She turned to the cooker, proud of herself – not for the lie, she had no sons, but for her acting ability under what she considered to be duress. She kept it up, feigning puzzlement when the doorbell rang. 'Help yourself to sugar,' she said airily.

'Markham?' Joff was on his feet as soon as he saw him. 'Have you found the bastard?'

'We'd like you to come with us. Down to the station.'

'What? Now?' He had only just noticed DC Hanson lurking in the background.

177

'Yes, now.'

Mrs Jordan said nothing but looked away, embarrassed when Joff caught her eye. He left without speaking but she only felt a twinge of conscience.

'What's this about?' Joff asked once he was in the back of the car, suspicion in his eyes when Markham got in the back with him.

'You'll find out soon enough.'

With less than five hours' sleep Ian was not at his best, and knowing what lay ahead didn't help. He waited impatiently until Joff was brought into the station and led down the corridor past an open door inside which Bilton-Jones sat facing outwards. Neither man showed any recognition of the other. Bilton-Jones was waiting for his lawyer to return; Joff was wondering if he needed one, but it didn't really matter either way, not now that Bilton-Jones had been caught.

Moira Roper's hands were on her slender hips as she surveyed the kitchen table which was laid, ready for a meal. Because she no longer baked and cooked as she had done when Mark was at home and before she got a job, she made an all-out effort one night of the week. This was a small sop to Ian who had always enjoyed her meat pies and cakes. It had done him no good, of course – he struggled to keep the pounds at bay but, all credit to him, he did not usually allow himself to be more than half a stone heavier than he liked to be.

At twelve she had left her office at the garage and come straight home to pick mint and runner beans from the garden. The recipe for beef with grapes and shallots was not one she had tried before but it sounded like Ian's sort of thing. The new potatoes had been scrubbed, the beans strung and the carrots scraped which meant they could eat around three, when Ian had promised to be home, or later that evening if that was not the case. 'I won't hold my breath,' Moira said as she turned down the heat under the beef stew to allow it to simmer.

She was thinking about the telephone call he had received the previous night and the one she had taken shortly afterwards from Lucy. Moira had been unable to avoid hearing Ian's tirade as he spoke to Barry; his temper was something they were used to and it was soon spent, but she had never heard him address a friend so. To compound the issue her conversation with Lucy had been strained.

'What's up with your husband?' Lucy had asked.

Moira almost said her phone bill wouldn't stand the length of time her answers would take but realised Lucy was not in the mood to be frivolous. 'I don't know. He stormed out in a filthy mood.' There wasn't much more she could add – although Ian confided in her as far as work was concerned, she knew better than to pass it on to others, even the wife of Ian's partner. Moira had quickly changed the subject and invited Lucy and Martin over on Sunday afternoon. 'Barry, too, if he's free. Just for a change of scenery,' she had added, knowing how grateful she had been to get out of the house when Mark was small. 'If Barry can't bring you, I'll pick you up about two, or will that interfere with his feeds?'

'You're joking. There's no such thing as routine in this house yet.'

Moira did not add that being married to a policeman there never would be. Lucy knew that already. Taking the remains of the red wine she had used in the casserole she went outside and sat in one of the garden chairs watching the bees at work. The street was remarkably peaceful and already she could smell the first hint of the night-scented stock in the border which later would be overpowering. Bill and Janice, next door, were making the most of the late summer afternoon; she could hear their muted voices through the lattice-work fence.

When she opened her eyes the angle of the sun had altered significantly. For over an hour she had slept undisturbed.

There was still no sign of Ian. It was another three hours before he did return.

10

Richard Fry had admitted his part in things. Yes, he drove Bilton-Jones around, yes, he suspected that the stops they made were to collect money and yes, he had provided the gun. He swore he did not know it was the same one which had killed the copper's wife nor its intended use.

'You're an accessory,' DC Craig Hanson told him. 'If someone asks you to provide a gun there's only one reason they want it.'

'I thought it was to frighten someone with.' But he hadn't, not really, not once he heard that Jasmine Grant had been shot dead.

His part was straightforward and he was duly charged although he might, because of his co-operation, get off more lightly than he deserved. He had made a list of their regular visits, adding that he only ever stayed in the car. DCI Roper had been pleased to note that the Taj Mahal was not one of them but what he did not know, nor ever found out, was that the pair of them enjoyed a free lunch every Thursday.

Roberts, Gregson and Sadiqi, when faced with the facts, held up their hands. Yes, they had each paid the man money until they were sick of it. The minute the payments stopped they had received a beating as a warning. Worse was to come if the payments were not resumed.

There were thirty different outlets. Officers would be sent to each. How relieved those businessmen and women would be. Ian was not sure how the CC would want to deal with things – they could, after all, be charged with obstruction by not having come forward. Time would tell. Time and the state of the CC's digestive system which played him up from time to time or, to quote him, 'gives me merry hell'.

Bilton-Jones had hidden behind the shield of his brief but it didn't matter that he wasn't talking – Fry had talked enough for both of them, as had Joff. He, too, had been charged. Mark Howard? Ian pondered. Well, it seemed he wasn't as stupid as he came across. If he had known what was occurring then he'd done well to avoid getting dragged in. He was in the clear. But what about Petesy French and his part in it? That still remained a mystery. Even the loquacious Fry couldn't explain it away. Someone could, but who? Not Petesy, that was for sure.

Ian's head thumped with lack of sleep and disgust. Joff was the next one to be interviewed and Ian didn't want to do it. He did not want to hear an officer admit he was bent. The man looks awful, Ian thought as he and Markham sat opposite him. There was no solicitor present; Joff had refused the services of one.

'Does the name Bilton-Jones mean anything to you?' Say no, Ian prayed, say no and make Richard Fry a liar.

'Yes. I know him.'

'In what capacity?'

'We met some years ago. His wife knew Jassy's parents.'

'So you only know him in a social capacity? Tell me about it.'

'We meet now and then and have a meal.'

'The four of you?' Ian watched him closely. Joff was trembling and avoiding his eyes. He had seen Bilton-Jones in the station, he must know it was over.

'No, the two of us.'

'A rather odd arrangement, isn't it? Joff, why don't you make it easy on yourself.'

The pause was long enough for Ian and Markham to think he wasn't going to say any more.

'It was for Jassy. She'd never have been able to live on my salary.'

'Did you ever try?'

Joff shook his head. 'I didn't want to subject her to that.'

It was hardly a pittance, Ian thought but did not say. 'How much? Over the years how much did Bilton-Jones pay you for beating up decent members of the public, and how much did you make of your own accord?'

He was defeated. Ian saw it as he asked the question, phrased in such a way as to make him more ashamed. Both officers held their breath in amazement at the figure Joff quoted. 'Who was the other one? The other man who helped you put the boot in?'

Joff looked genuinely surprised at this. 'No one,' he said, meeting Ian's eyes for the first time. 'We always worked alone. We took it in turns.' Ian felt sick when he named another officer.

'Two of the victims said there were two men.' But even as he spoke Ian realised what had happened. Gregson and Roberts had not been honest. Big men that they were, neither had been prepared to admit he had received such a beating from a single person. That could be dealt with later. They had one confession, now they needed to know about Jassy. But this was a game Joff wasn't prepared to play. He stuck to his story, and was unable to shed any light on her murder.

Bilton-Jones had been in the pub, as had Richard Fry. Each was trying to blame the other or Joff now they couldn't pin it on French.

It was late afternoon before Ian decided they had all had enough. The three men were to be held overnight. There had been no problems with that as it was agreed that their part in the murder was still in question. Feeling grubby inside and out, Ian drove home wanting nothing more than a bath and a beer.

It was rarely that Moira worried for the safety of her husband. A long time had elapsed since he had patrolled the streets or put himself in physical danger but this situation was differ-

182

ent. A policeman's wife had been killed and possibly by someone involved in protection. Dangerous people, she thought as she turned off the gas and poked the beef with a fork. It almost fell to bits.

Restless and trying not to admit to worry, she moved from room to room then back to the garden where she tried to read but found herself dead-heading flowers and pulling up the odd weed. It was with a sigh of relief that she recognised the sound of the car engine as Ian pulled up outside 14 Belmont Terrace. Moira followed him into the kitchen.

White-faced and wordlessly Ian opened the fridge and pulled out a can of beer. He poured it steadily but it took an effort. 'Is there enough hot water for a bath?'

'Yes.' Disappointed because he had led her to believe that all the ends would have been tied up by lunchtime, she knew there was no point in complaining or asking him what had gone wrong. In half an hour she would take him up another drink and hope that it would loosen his tongue a little. 'Some way to spend Saturday night,' she muttered as she heard his heavy tread on the stairs. There was no point either in asking what time he wanted to eat, a grunt would be the best she could hope for by way of a reply.

'Thanks, love,' he said when she handed him a second glass of Adnams. The bathroom was full of steam, his clothes were strewn on the floor and she would later find wet towels added to the pile. Biting her tongue she went back downstairs to wait.

'You look better.' He did. Colour had returned to his face and he had washed away some of the strain.

'I feel it. I'm having another drink. Want one? Or we could pop out if you fancy it?'

Moira no longer knew what she wanted to do. 'Yes,' she surprised herself by saying. 'Let's go out. Will I need a jacket?'

'No, I shouldn't think so.'

Ian had put on casual trousers and a short-sleeved shirt, one of his smarter outfits. If she stopped to clear up the bathroom or to change out of the jeans she had put on when she came in from the garden Ian would flop into a chair and fall asleep. She picked up her bag and said she was ready.

The sky was low and grey and the evening was humid but by the time they reached the Green and the Crown was in sight a breeze had quickened and a few spots of rain hit the ground. 'Some detective,' Moira said with a smile. 'You said I didn't need a jacket.'

'It's warm rain,' he laughed.

The Crown was busy and had a Saturday night atmosphere so different from any other night of the week. The lattice windows were open, the chintz curtains beginning to stir. Unusually there was no sign of Bob Jones, the landlord. He had taken Connie out to some brewery do.

Ian bought the drinks and turned to the doorway. 'False alarm,' he said. The dark blobs the size of a one penny piece were already beginning to dry up. 'Shall we sit outside?'

This was so unlike Ian that Moira followed him across the grass to a wooden slatted bench which circled the huge tree in the middle of the Green without replying. It was obvious he wanted to talk and the crowded lounge bar of the Crown was not the place to do it.

'Ah, that's better.' He had sluiced down a third of his pint before setting the glass carefully on the ground. Moira waited.

'We thought Joff'd done it. Killed his wife. In a way he did – well, as good as.' He closed his eyes as if it was all too much to contemplate. 'He'd abused his position, you see. He'd got into something he couldn't find a way out of. The harder he tried to extricate himself the deeper in he got.'

'Protection?'

'Mm. He got to know a man named Bilton-Jones through Jassy's parents. The Goodwins knew his wife otherwise I doubt they'd have had anything to do with him. Anyway, they met at some social function. Bilton-Jones needed some muscle, someone to do the dirty work. He knew, too, that Jassy was expected to live on her husband's salary and that Joff never felt he was good enough for her.'

184

'Hang on, are you saying he did it to keep her happy? I didn't know her very well but she didn't strike me as that sort.'

'We'll never know for certain, but I think it relates more to Bilton-Jones's own situation.'

'How do you mean?'

'His wife's got all the connections, been to the right schools, you know the sort of thing. He tried to keep up with her. I think he found it easy to convince Joff that a woman like Jassy wouldn't be happy without all the trappings and maybe he was right. She didn't want to grow up, we know that much.'

'And she didn't want to get a job. But surely she questioned where the money was coming from? I know the house was paid for but it would still take a lot of upkeep, and her clothes and everything.'

'You've hit the proverbial nail there, Moira. Jassy wasn't stupid. Like her parents she believed that Joff had some sort of private income. I know, it sounds impossible but not all partners discuss their finances openly and they had separate bank accounts. She found out by chance that something was wrong. She opened one of his letters by mistake. He swears it was a mistake, that she had never done that before, and I believe him. It was a statement of sorts, addressed to J. Grant. Anyway, she questioned him about the large amounts paid in and he more or less admitted what he was up to. She took it badly and . . .'

'And I don't blame her. I think I'd leave you if you ever did anything like that. Not that you would,' she amended hastily, knowing how touchy Ian was over such things. 'Not many people could live with that knowledge, not when your husband's a police officer. So, what happened?'

'She gave him an ultimatum, pretty similar to the one you just offered me. Only she also said she would go to his chief superintendent as well if he didn't pack it in.'

'But he didn't.'

'He'd got this fishing trip lined up, it had been arranged

some time ago. He needed time on his own to think what to do. Before he went he spoke to Bilton-Jones, mistakenly thinking him to be a reasonable man. He said he wanted out, that his wife had found out and wasn't prepared to put up with it. Bilton-Jones couldn't afford to let him go. Not only was he the muscle he needed for keeping his sources of income under control, he had also discovered that Joff was running his own little game.'

'Oh, no.'

'Joff told us that he thought he could get away from Bilton-Jones, that he could honestly say so to Jassy . . .'

'And continue taking money himself? Oh, Ian, how awful. So who did kill her?'

'We don't know. We know everything else but we don't know that. Joff's alibi checks out.' Ian shrugged. Prangnell had been more than useful. He had put them on to the taxi driver who had driven Joff to Edinburgh. True, Joff hadn't eaten breakfast: he'd gone for a long walk to get things straight in his head before he returned home. He had been seen by one or two people who could bear this out. A man fitting his description and carrying a hold-all had been offered a lift by a couple of tourists but he had turned it down. Ian's theory about the trains had been way off the mark.

'Well, this Bilton-Jones seems the most likely candidate if he thought Jassy was going to drop them all in it.'

'I know. But what puzzles me is why? With Jassy dead what possible hold did he have over Joff?'

'Beats me, Ian. Can I get you another drink? Only one more, mind, then we'll go home to eat.' Moira stood and picked up their glasses, chewing her lip as she went in to get them refilled. It looked very much as if Sunday was going to be ruined too. At least she'd have Lucy and Martin for company.

The sun was shining but with none of the fierceness of the last two months. Moira and Lucy sat on a blanket on the lawn with Martin between them as he slept protected by a cotton hat and an umbrella Moira had fixed in place with a couple of metal spikes driven into the lawn. A yard or so away Barry, in white shorts and a polo shirt, was lying with his hands behind his head, apparently also asleep as he listened to his wife and her friend quietly chatting. Beside him was a glass of beer, warm now. He was not officially part of the murder team but half of his mind was at the station as he wondered how Ian was getting on. He had not wanted to be at the station and he wasn't sure what he was doing at the Ropers' house either, because he had not forgiven Ian for his suspicions. They had not yet had the chance to talk about it.

'Anyone for a cup of tea?'

'Love one, thanks,' Barry said, without opening his eyes. 'Oh, you did say beer, didn't you?' Moira grinned. Not asleep after all, she thought. Martin began to stir. His cheeks were flushed with sleep. 'I'll heat up a bottle,' she called from the doorway.

It was Moira who sat in a deck chair and fed him, the feel of his tiny warm body bringing back memories she had thought would never resurface. How long ago it seemed since Mark was that small. It was in that position that Ian came across the party, a cameo of happy families.

'Hello.' Moira smiled, making no comment about the greyness of her husband's skin nor the fact that the stubble was showing because he had gone in without shaving that morning. 'Here he is, say hello to Martin Ian Swan.'

'Has he finished the bottle?'

'Just about.'

Ian waited until Martin made it clear that he was not interested in the last half-inch, puckering his mouth and pushing his tongue against the teat. 'Can I?' He looked to Lucy for permission. She nodded.

'You'd better wind him.' Moira handed over the child, amused at the awkward way in which Ian handled him until he had him settled against his wide shoulder, one hand around his back the other tentatively patting it. 'He won't break,' Moira commented with another smile.

Ian was rewarded by a couple of burps which made them all laugh. It was strange, he thought, how such behaviour in a baby was considered to be amusing but from an adult would be deemed rude. 'Any of that tea going?' He raised his eyebrows. 'I know how women's-libbish you've become but you can see that I'm otherwise occupied.'

'Any excuse.' Moira hesitated before asking the question to which she dreaded hearing the answer. 'Ian, will you be going in again tonight?'

'No. Not tonight. Nor tomorrow or Tuesday.'

Moira nodded and went back to the kitchen. It was over, then.

'It's over? Barry, who had been leaning on one elbow, sat up, knowing as Moira had done that the case was at an end.

Ian nodded. 'It's over. And I might take early retirement.'

'Pigs might fly.'

'You'll be sorry when I shout, "Duck, here comes a pig."'

Barry produced a packet of cigarettes and offered one to Ian. On the pretext of not wishing to smoke near the baby, Ian handed Martin back to his mother and the two men strolled to the end of the garden. 'Want to talk about it?' Barry asked.

'Not particularly, but you want to hear about it.' Briefly he explained the part of the three men in terrorising local businesses to pay out money but Barry knew most of it already.

'He did it, you know. Joff did it.'

'What? I thought they were the ideal couple.'

'So did most people. He married her for her money. It was as simple as that. So sodding banal it makes me want to weep. The Goodwins always suspected that this was the case but they couldn't talk their daughter out of it.'

'Didn't they suspect him of killing her?' Barry ground out his cigarette in Ian's lawn. He was no longer enjoying it.

'No. There was no reason to. After all, there wasn't any money, only the house. To someone like Joff that wouldn't

188

have been enough to kill for. He killed her to stop her coming to us. Despite his initial statement he had no intention of giving up an easy living. He had created an image and he had to live up to it.'

'You'll have to explain because I'm not getting any of this.'

'The fishing trip was a cover, an alibi planned in advance – '

'But – '

Ian held up a hand. 'Wait a minute. I know you're going to say he didn't have an alibi for the time when he could have travelled back and killed her – well, he wouldn't have had one unless we found the taxi driver and the tourist couple. He meant it to be that way, he knew an innocent man didn't *need* an alibi. However, he was clever enough to realise that the village nearest the place he was staying only had two taxis. The driver would remember him, Joff would have known that.'

'So how did he do it?'

'Simple. Simple when you know he'd planned it in advance with Bilton-Jones. The latter arranged for Fry to get hold of a gun in return for which Joff was to pay Fry via Bilton-Jones. Joff had the gun with him when he went away. In case we checked further he was actually on the train on which he'd booked a seat but what we didn't know was that Bilton-Jones had hired a car, in his own name, using his own licence, and driven it to London to a pre-arranged place. Joff got straight off the train and drove to Rickenham knowing that something would've been slipped into French's drink. We gather it was probably a couple of Mrs Bilton-Jones's sleeping tablets.

'Joff goes home and kills his wife then drives into Saxborough Road where he waits for Petesy to leave the pub. As we thought, he calls out to him offering him a lift. Petesy accepts. He knows Joff by sight because he's seen him on one occasion with Bilton-Jones. Joff's fairly safe in the hired car but if anyone does think they recognise him he had proof he was on the train. He drives back to Colchester, leaves the car to

189

be collected and boards the local train back, guessing one of us will be there to meet him.'

'They cold-bloodedly planned that, then tried to pin it on French? God, they're despicable. So he ran him out to the end of Maple Grove and left him there.'

'Precisely. The tablets had taken full effect by then. After several pints of cider he would seem as if he was drunk.'

'Who made the phone call?'

'We don't know. Joff, maybe, or Bilton-Jones from the pub, the phone's out the back.'

'Ironic, isn't it? He didn't kill her for her money, he killed her because there wasn't any.'

'You may call it ironic, I think it's indescribable.'

'Ian – '

'I think I know what you're going to say and I'm sorry, Barry. You see, I wasn't sure how many people were involved – one other, as it happens – but I had to be certain you weren't involved. You know tact isn't always my strong point.'

'You can say that again.'

Moira was watching them with her arms folded. 'Your wife's ready to go home and your son's ready for bed. I've ordered a taxi.'

'They're going to love us. ' It had been a struggle getting there with all the baby stuff although they hadn't bothered with a pram. Knowing the Ropers' generous hospitality with drinks they had not dared to risk the car. Even Lucy had enjoyed a couple of glasses of the wine which had made her feel sick during her pregnancy.

'It gets easier,' Moira commented wryly. 'Have you heard any more about a transfer?'

There was an uncomfortable pause and Ian's eyes narrowed. This was it then. Barry would be leaving them.

'Yes. I'll be based in Gloucester.'

Gloucester. It was the other side of the country. Ian and Moira would both miss their friends and miss seeing Martin

190

Ian growing up. 'Progress,' Ian hissed as Lucy called from the kitchen doorway.

'Barry? Are you ready? The taxi's here.' The detachable car-seat was in her hand with the baby safely strapped in.

'Coming.' He turned back to Ian. 'Well, at least you can relax for the next couple of days. Look, why don't you come over to dinner one night? We can tell you all our plans.'

I don't want to know, Ian thought, but caught Moira's eye just in time before he said anything.

'We'd love to.' Moira kissed the sleeping child and walked with them to the waiting taxi. Ian still looked strained but it would pass. A couple of days with the house to himself would take care of that.

'How about if your wife offers to buy you a drink? It'll be the second one in two days, you realise.'

'Do you know, that's one of the nicest things you've ever said to me.' He put an arm across her narrow shoulders and felt the warmth of her body through her T-shirt.

Moira grinned. 'I'll just put a dress on.'

'You look fine like that to me.' His eyes rested on her legs beneath the shorts.

'No way am I walking down the road like this.'

He could not understand her. Most women would have been only too proud to show off legs like hers. But there were a lot of things about that day he was unable to understand. There were, he reflected, many things about life he didn't understand.

She left him for a few minutes to go and change and he was filled with sadness, wondering how any man could harm the woman he had married and why so many things had to change. But a couple of pints of Adnams and a slap-up curry in the Taj Mahal would go a long way towards making the world seem all right again. Moira came downstairs wearing a cotton dress. She had put on some lipstick, taken her hair from the band which had held it in a pony-tail and sprayed on some perfume. They set out together, locking the door behind them with no comment from Ian about the days when this action was not necessary.

Taking her completely by surprise Ian reached for her hand as they walked down the quiet summer streets to the Crown. He was, he thought, a very lucky man. Being married to Moira compensated for the down side of the career he had chosen but which, despite days like today, he would not be without.

Oh, Joff, he thought, you got yourself on a roller-coaster you couldn't get off. Ian realised sadly that beneath the likeable, heroic, affluent exterior lay a deep-seated greed and desperate need for admiration, that Joff Grant would not have been able to survive as a lesser man in the eyes of his wife or his colleagues. For that simple reason he had killed her.

Enough, he told himself as Moira looked up at him and squeezed his hand. But he really did wish that Barry wasn't leaving.